经 典 照 亮 前 程

[美] 弗罗斯特·甘德　著
Forrest Gander
李　栋　译

BE WITH

相伴

华东师范大学出版社
·上海·

图书在版编目（CIP）数据

相伴 /（美）弗罗斯特·甘德著；李栋译. —— 上海：华东师范大学出版社，2020（独角兽文库）
ISBN 978-7-5760-0111-2

Ⅰ.①相… Ⅱ.①弗…②李… Ⅲ.①诗集－美国－现代 Ⅳ.① I712.25

中国版本图书馆 CIP 数据核字 (2020) 第 036989 号

上海市版权局著作权合同登记 图字：09 - 2019 - 699 号

相　伴

著　　者	[美] 弗罗斯特·甘德	门市（邮购）电话	021-62869887
译　　者	李　栋	门市地址	上海市中山北路 3663 号华东师
策划编辑	许　静		范大学校内先锋路口
责任编辑	朱晓韵	网　　店	http://hdsdcbs.tmall.com
审读编辑	陈　斌		
责任校对	时东明	印刷者	上海中华商务联合印刷有限公司
装帧设计	卢晓红	开　　本	850 × 1168 32 开
封面插图	Rodrigo Corral	印　　张	7
摄影插图	Michael Flomen	字　　数	111 千字
		版　　次	2021 年 1 月第 1 版
出版发行	华东师范大学出版社	印　　次	2021 年 1 月第 1 次
社　　址	上海市中山北路 3663 号	书　　号	ISBN 978-7-5760-0111-2
邮　　编	200062	定　　价	65.00 元
网　　址	www.ecnupress.com.cn		
电　　话	021-60821666	出 版 人	王　焰
行政传真	021-62572105		
客服电话	021-62865537		

（如发现本版图书有印订质量问题，请寄回本社
客服中心调换或电话 021-62865537 联系）

弗罗斯特·甘德

我出生在莫哈韦沙漠。我去过也写过很多别的沙漠，如利比亚的撒哈拉、中国的戈壁、智利的阿塔卡马、美国的索诺拉、印度的塔尔等。像空白的一页，沙漠让我彻底谦卑。我所做的一切都不能让沙漠或是文学那一页变得更好。

我和一位伟大的诗人 C. D. 莱特一起生活了三十多年。她是我见过的最具美德、慷慨、诚实、热心的人。我们在物质世界里的感官生活和书本里的精神世界不可分割。

我成年的大部分时间里都对翻译着迷。即使在小时候，我的阅读也很国际化；翻译过来的童话和神话培养了我的想象力。

中国的古典诗词对我的影响巨大。近二十年来，我有幸推介过一批中国当代诗人的翻译。我（跟人）合译过日本诗人吉增刚造和野村喜和夫的作品，还翻译过许多拉丁美洲和西班牙诗人，尤其是西班牙语女诗人的作品。

我一直对和其他领域的艺术家合作有兴趣，如电影、摄影、陶艺和雕塑等。我觉得这种合作就是我所希望的开放敏感地生存在这世上的方式。

我以为你是漂流世界的锚；

但不是这样：哪里都没有锚。

漂流世界里没有锚。糟糕。

我以为你是。糟糕。漂流的世界。

——威廉·布朗克

目录

CONTENTS

相伴

政治从亲密间开始

儿子

被遮住的不是镜子，而是
我们之间还没能说出口的话。为什么

要说什么死，或是必然，
说什么身体是怎样指挥无数的蠕虫

就好像这只是可以消化的概念，而不是
一个活生生、优美的个体？就让这成为

一首挽歌，或是你我痛苦的
记录。似乎是某种自轻。

所以我们继续看着无头的太阳醒来，树木
继续让我恶心。善的核心

有着自己的一套基因。你的膝盖弯曲处
挂着一个细菌群，我的胃肠里

蠕动的寄生虫在穿行。有谁只是他们自己？
我和你妈妈年经的时候，在大莱波蒂斯撞见

神像的脸和脚都被人肆意破坏，不过
没有人敢碰那一排守护者美杜莎的头像。

她说话的时候，你妈妈说话的时候，就算
牵着的灰狗都会被震住。我被她震住。

我把一生都给了陌生人，没能给我爱的人。
她唯一的血脉，她的血只在你身体里流淌。

招魂

这时我的悲音跳出了语言。

像一群漂流的蜜蜂。

这时接着重重的沉默。

我被蜜蜂击晕,失去意识。

这时也没有我的出路。

这时我半浑半噩地活着,梦见我还醒着,

躲避朋友,呕吐不停,在脸上手臂上一根根地拔刺。

这时她的声音固定在了蒸气色的背景上。

这时沙丘鹤的尾羽亮了。

这时我苏醒过来,知道得付全程接送费。

这时司机转过头来说,弄垮你的

也不一定是你的错。

这时没有任何征兆，

他开始吹奏秃鹫骨头做成的笛子。

这时我老了，就像又一次用我的双手掰开蜂巢。

这时我幻想一个比人生更真实的空间。

这时至少还有某种可能。

某种……我不相信的可能。

墓志铭

写下你
存在了我
不会仅仅是
失聪的翻译。

因为这个段落
没有续篇，当
我看到——就如你
永远不会再
被人看到——你看着我
就如我永远
不会再被人看到

现在我站立在
荣耀的宝座前，文字
必须被隐藏。在哪里，
如果不是话语本身呢?

天生迟钝又
失明，被职责
圈住，意识到

内心野兽的

凝视，我

躲在各式

工具般的存在后

就如躲在——广场的

鳄鱼鳞甲后面——

此时氰化物

从云边飘到

水边。这里

似乎也能看到

排成的

人行，

又一个亲密得

致命的、我们

共生的手势。

尽管我也把生命

慢慢磨成死亡，我

带来的丑恶

比我活得长久。

寂寥

一

他拿出了烟筒，随即颤栗
屈于它的仁慈又把控着它

塞黑唇牛蛇把密封玻璃罩提起
从嘴角到通风口大约三英尺六

热血青年隐喻着死亡
他们又有什么线索

她的味道：醋、氧化锌、扁柏
他醒着梦到过梦里也梦到

再看一季《浴血黑帮》
这让他镶的牙疼

而现在他患上了勃起功能障碍
我也是，灰尘说

摩托车停在残疾车位

他注视着挺立的枯立木森林

二

热血青年隐喻着死亡
这让他镶的牙疼

塞黑唇牛蛇把密封玻璃罩提起
他醒着梦到过梦里也梦到

他拿出了烟筒，随即颤栗
我也是，灰尘说

从嘴角到通风口大约三英尺六
而现在他患上了勃起功能障碍

她的味道：醋、氧化锌、扁柏
屈于它的仁慈又把控着它

他们又有什么线索
他注视着挺立的枯立木森林

再看一季《浴血黑帮》
摩托车停在残疾车位

碳化森林

星期五还睁着的眼睛。

预兆和预兆剥下的皮。一圈圈的肉

蜂拥而下。像一园蚂蟥

丢下某个未点燃的灾难。

满身荆棘的幽灵直立在那里，漆黑一片。

谁说道，这是不可译的世界。

盖在形式的尖顶上。

深渊降临。碎片溅射。

而你本以为的深色长尾鳕般的光辉

其实是剃下的熊毛

熊在生锈的笼子里挤着胆汁。巢

筑在柔和的半透明声音之间

从你嘴唇上掉下的

是某人呼吸的印迹。

情理

你能看到：她的　　　　　　　　　　意识在她的皮肤里
而他主要的材料　　　　　　　　　　　是失重状态
在佩特卢马家禽农场她　　　照光检查鸡蛋
做白日梦　　　　　　梦见星星虎视眈眈
在斑节虾星云的紫外线照射下
他看见了自己　　　　　一个地方的受害者
在光着膀子的神之间　　　　　在草坪上玩飞盘
啊死亡，他（睡时）喃喃自语，我　　　找你来了
是真的，生命　　　　反复无常
充满欢乐　　　　　和困惑
就像苏　　　　蕙的回文诗

有一次喝　　　　　　　　　水时他咳了，
她开始　　　　大笑，误解了他的手势
每件事都把失去的　　　　拖在身后

　　　　　　　黑暗，变亮吧
　　　　　　我脑海中有龙葵

他们本要把照着夕阳的门　　　　　　关上
但她的膝盖　　　　　　戳破了肥皂泡

而他在外面待了很久　　　　　　　　仰面躺着
在斑节虾星云的紫外线照射下

在合上的窗帘　　　　后面
护士　　　　　　　　咒骂
表达　　　　　　　　他的不善言辞
创伤　　　　　　　　带来它独有的清晰。
在他的眼里　　　　　每个人都看到她
他拿出一支烟　　　　给狗吃
回去接着　　　　　　计算节拍

又回到　　　　　　　　常见的朋友间互无消息
嘀嗒糖　　　　　　　在他口袋里碰撞
他嘴里满是龙舌兰酒味　　早上九点就抽烟
不可读但不　　　　　　　　模棱两可
像猎犬　　　　　　　向着地平线咆哮
在斑节虾星云的紫外线照射下

她写到，生命　　　　　在语言里感受生命
她丰腴的思维　　　　　　　　　　如此充盈
形容词　　　　　　　发出嘶嘶声响而消失
他观察着　　　　　　被虚无投下的
影子被他自己的　　　　　　虚无投下

《分娩圣母》

然后闻到它，

感受它，

声音还未传到

他耳边，他跪在

悬崖边，第一次

回过头，朝向

此时清晰可见的瀑布

在四百多米长的高地喷涌——

花岗岩横跨山谷

他停顿了一下，

垂下眼睛

凝视了片刻，难以

承受这片

安宁——广袤、自由

骇人又原始。这条

赤裸的河流

被推上

断层的祭坛，

弯腰的柏树

聚集在发光的岩石两侧，

当他蹒跚着，腿脚发麻，

想站起来时——树影间

一道裂隙，霓虹变幻

在无尽的爆裂中

蒸发消逝。

感于费尔南达·梅尔彻[1]的一句话

你的生活里闹了什么鬼？

在我身上发生过的最糟糕的事？

忙得昏乱，我压碎自己的生命让它坠落

接着我比自己的命活得更久，在我的痛苦上

潇洒，像风中的柏树。我看着

星星从一只黑色的鸡蛋里冒出。明澈的

损失。有人来跟我说天花板角落里

我桌子上方长腿颤抖的

蜘蛛现在并不存在。它被夹在

暴力般不可停滞的

一天的时间里和我在内心发现的

空虚里。前额绷紧着自怜。

我说，你以为你了解我，但你

不过是道听途说。而她说，

我了解你，你也就那么回事。

1　费尔南达·梅尔彻（1982—　　），墨西哥青年女作家。

走出光明

漂白
树干间的
空白，雾
在一大片绿中
勾勒出
斜坡上
每棵松树的
轮廓。

也许就是这样，
只是一直以来
被什么遮掩了？
着急，分心？雾。
一棵松。带着疑问的
黄昏雀。什么
变了。你发现
到了一个自己
并不期待的、另一个
世界，你看到
你自己还是
门外的

狼群。门

虚掩，目瞪口呆地看着你自己的
门。你像绞肉机复活人
冲了进去，
你挖出
得罪了你的
右眼。你像大骗子
冲进来
吞食
你自己的肉
还像永不
放手那般，撕裂
你的肌腱，咬
你的股骨。你忍
不住冲进来，
撞见你自己
一个人，脆弱，
在你垂死的隐私中，
弯腰用纸巾
捡起卧室地板上

一只被压碎的蜘蛛，
半知半觉地感受到腹腔

神经丛里还不能

被理解的力，发现

自己似乎

又一次存在于

某种物体的内部

就像一个方程式的

余数，赎罪的祭品，

提醒着和解的

不可能——

和解什么？再一次。原谅

你自己吧，他们说，但

原谅你

所经历的事之后，

还有什么被留下？你不可能

在不断淋下的时刻间

抛开当下的

沙漏

甚至不可能

把某个超级地下网络间

碎步快行蚂蚁

留下的踪迹

和星光照耀下

碎裂星系的遗迹

区分开。你想

是该关上门了
但你的脸变了，
那么多的鱼尾纹。你
一定是
进入了下一个阶段
你开始
认清
你凡人的身躯，
你和世界
各种各样的关联，就像
一个所有你并不
知道却已接受的
事物的仓库，人
或是非人的，一切
都冲涨着情感、一触即发
这也解释了你双手的
颤抖，就像现在
你觉察到
你身体里的那个躯体——
就像静止的
挂铃
揪住、聚积

周围每个幽灵般的

颤动。

听起来像什么

当种子在片岩中分类

被称为黑狗水银的林地标志山靛

像液岩在流动

像蓝墙上白点黑色的蜥蜴粪便

一种所有别的失去都能套进去的失去

拨弄一颗痣直到流血

当一天在假意的决心之上向前推进

如果不是并置，她问道，那什么是联系的桥梁？

想把词定在"感情经历"上总是令人发毛

蔚蓝色的长脚金龟、石蚕、蜂虱、斑蝥、刺椿象

反责蜂拥围着落日

除此周围一片静寂

被给予了一辈子的你，又拿生命做了什么？

曾经坚实的房子

厨房里唱歌的声音　　　　不是你的
厨房里　　　　没有唱歌的声音

打开昨晚的　　　　比萨饼盒子
干了　　　　奶酪丝拉开
像压坏的、手里的　　　　肌腱

从你的深处我溢入　　　　浅水
扭动　　　　窒息
我的语言　　　　爆裂

我多希望　　　　你在这儿
我试着　　　　收集边缘
所有给我们留下　　　　印象的地方
所有的都回来了　　　　像雾气般奇异
升起了又平躺　　　　在桥下

当你要求少一些　　　　严密多一些情理
当你要　　　　求多一些——

认知：并非背诵　　　　而是像

卸下　　　　　　　　躯体的事件

尽管现在我　　　　　　所有的回忆都从结果开始

像菲尔多西的　　　　　《列王纪》

我们的编年史融入风景　　　　　旧事发生的地方

主角如此松散　　　　　他们的分子

和一片片水域　　　　　和大地和光混合

因为就如他们所说　　　　　人当然是草

即使这里　　　　　　　在蛇岛

没有苦涩　　　　　　　没有嫉妒没有贪婪

除非　　　　　　　　另外还有什么

近似于就拿着　　　　　一根木掀翻开落叶

却找到了一条　　　　　鲜亮的蝮蛇

探听

什么东西合上便

发光？什么打开

就变暗？你又

绊倒在哪里？

这紫罗兰的

灭绝。你的嘴唇上

还留有泡沫。

上午 8 点 16 分。早晨

昏睡的脸上

一百万双眼

在翻滚。迁徙的鸟群

似你般的物种

白热化

渐渐透明。

一位观鸟者举起了

她的双筒望远镜。这连续

不断的有或者没有

你的词语

将你定在这里

（这里＜的这里＞）即使

你满是怀疑地

敲打你的双眼。那些

你喜欢的声音（人类的

或是别的），你能

听到它们的回音

嘶嘶作响

就像钉锤打在

铁匠铁砧上

烙下的

火红的印？

那些声音

背后，又是什么

如黑雨般

冲开

你耳朵的阀门，

不是一股股洪流，

而是慢慢地

停息不止地

从各处涌来的

毫无懈怠。

第一首叙事诗：花环
仿圣十字若望

太初有道	宛如沉浸
幸福之中	道无尽享有
同一道词	据说开始
没有起始	继续向前
一笔弹撞	穿越炽烈虚空
因为道	至始
总是	孕育
聚集其	后果
为道的荣耀	抓住生命
及从道中收来	生命所有物质
爱于人被爱于	人如此类推
而缠绕他们的爱	归一
总结两个	声音一个被爱
两人之中	每个个体间

同一幸福　　　　使其成为同一情人
没有坦白的光　　　　辉——灿烂

两人聚于一体　　　　个体拥有
个体于爱中　　　　道的全部

其每一生命　　　　缠绕于人
理解之外　　　　无法打开的结

如此炽烈的爱　　　　把两人缠绕
两人拥有同一声音　　　　世界的全部
爱愈是同一　　　　就愈有爱

古老的手磨石

手掌大小的一块玄武岩

（微观）小孔里

绿玉米、马齿苋

（蛇油）和松子的残迹

与烂的根

和杂草花粉（赭石粉）

混合，整个夏天

飘散开来

飘进一位跪着的妇女的

头皮（意图）在明亮的

石盆前她弯下了腰

松了松筋骨

斜方肌到

肱三头肌，手腕　　（像你的那样纤细）

轻轻转动

一圈，手——

磨石追着

手掌的

弧线（杯状）

她躯干的重量

下坠，此时

燕子下潜

沿着陡峭的

悬崖，她擦破的

温暖的手掌根

（金星丘）

压下来

发出尖锐的呼叫

石头和手

合二为一

轮子般

磨着，

制作者（气若

游丝）在她的工具里（轻盈）

生龙活虎

操心焦虑

她的头发垂下

遮住她

（像你的秀发）　　发光的双眼——　　（在你眼里）

欢快地，树影摩挲间

进入了这种节奏

是插曲

慢节奏间

她的孩子哭了

她摇着他

她所有的

　呼吸快慢

　　她的体态　　　　　　　　（呼吸）

　　　数不尽的（一呼一吸）

　　　　满负荷的分贝

　　　　　一日日的表达

　　　　　　压力，这一切

　　　　　　　压（向玄武岩），

　　　　　　　　水泡进了石头

　　　　　　　　　进入了（带孔的）石头

　　　　　　　　一缕兔毛

　　　　　　　从手上滑过

　　　　　　在眼睛发直的傍晚

　　　　　手分离了

　　　　兔子的毛发

　　　红蚂蚁从岩石土壤的

　　　洞穴中蜂拥而出

　　　钻过毛茸茸的草丛

　　　（直愣愣的蚂蚁）冲向

　　一个花园，那里

　三只火鸡啄着（食

草的）蚂蚁（所以

花园绿了）

一场小小的胜利

记录在

这个女人的　　　（你的双眼）

眼里　　　（她双眼的背后）

她磨着

石头上的石头

在洪水暴戾

怒吼间

在光阴里

时间收了她的光

在我（我们）的光里

我的瞳孔收缩了

它的镜头，而我在一片空地

弯下腰　　　（主，我跪下

在你的石头前）　去捡起

和掂量这份挚烈

老鹰滑翔展开双翼

我的手握紧

千年以前

她的手曾握住的

她慢慢消逝间

我清醒了（为

谁？）在一壑

绿绿的山丘上

有人跪下

在这一刻（甚至

现在）于我们

（静静流淌的）视线之外

跟他们说不

像某个

刚出现的

事物，他抓紧

她

直到

他四肢的

几丁质变硬

而他眼中

和他

翅膀

骨架间

流动的

液体

结晶了。

人类美好的
生活又是
怎样的。在
床笫间或
之外。极端的
结合。

当我打湿的脸颊
第一次在乳液中
打转，这把光亮的
獾毛刷
是你
给我的礼物，它
惊人的野生麝香味
锁在了我的脸上。

一上午的雾，斑驳的
山顶下面，一抹
奇异、灰色的帽带，
它的上缘滑向
南边而佩特卢马
奶厂轻细的
蒸汽正朝着一个方向
涌去。

不是
相较于一种幸福
选择另一种，而是
继续选择
阿波麦托克斯县府的
不幸福?

再次跌跌撞撞

默默地

回家，走进

我自己的

一行叩问。

被带得太远

迷失了方向？就像

携带着

黄蜂蛆的

毛毛虫变成

黄蜂蛆

咖喱烹调

毛毛虫的

尸体。

多么艰难——不

管表达得

如何糟糕——

你自己的或是

别人的痛苦，

被剥下外衣——转

　　　　　　身走开。

柜子

门吱呀作响

扬抑抑格式的评论：

幸福？

不过，每天早晨

都是一样的

场景。一只蜥蜴

在同一块

炙热的岩石上

做着俯卧撑。

我无法自拔的

倾向是

工作日常。

和最确切的
隐喻
差得不远：
一支雪茄
在火车站的
厕所里
裂开。

人类美好的
生活又是
怎样的。极端的
结合。

她说苦难是没必要的。

他说这是途径。

她说把它拖回原处。

她说你叫谁都是宝贝。

他说这有点像掉下的馅饼。

她说他说是为了能站在这儿。

意思就是

感觉上的

意思。

他们家犬深深的凝视，
她的胃咯咯叫着。
阴蒂在压力下勃起。
那是他额头上的瘤吗？
医生办公室里长长的下午
耗尽了她的生命。蜂鸟？
他的麂皮夹克上衣领颜色变深
是她头发上的油。

然后用牙齿
磨伤我的胳膊，
划开蛋壳的
一头
取出识别的幼虫
放进我的
嘴里。

要分解

它，由自我

导入。

我是谁就是

我能做什么。

在某一刻，变化

导致倒退，

大脑看成

是失败。恶心的

异味被培养出来。所以

带着档案般的

粗暴，我搜寻

你的脸，就像

追着共鸣的一边。

他的
腹腔里，
电梯缆线
断了。
此时我在
夜晚躺下，
她说，
我的心
悸动。

我采摘的
太晚的花
在花瓶里
嘶嘶作响，
想念着你。

当所要求的

是彻底的

改变

以至于

只有另一个

人格才有可能

成就它。

什么无明又恼人的

下颌自动的头颅

在咀嚼着我们以为

可以引我们

回到床上的

丝线?

你是
气喘吁吁了吗？
她在
隔壁
喊着。

贴上的
对话式的
回复。

大步飞奔又转身，

大步飞奔又转身，大步

飞奔又转身

回看

那条路

她站在那里

纹丝不动，就

像在看着什么。

我脑子里

有龙葵吗？

我设想

你带来的后果

是我生活需求的

某个阶段？

亲爱的蜘蛛，在
这个家里，八条
腿太多了。

几天后
他们极乐之福上
长出了一层坚不可摧的
皮肤。之后又自己
完全溶解了，
皮肤的液体
成分成了
一种啫喱
一个新生物
从其间爆发出来
它的器官
没有任何
和之前事物
相认同的迹象。

我做过

什么傻事吗?

我是不是

不用负责任的

胆小鬼?

悬空在

南北

之间,

说是激励着

疼痛,

却也由此

维系着

乐队式的

张力。

饱和点。
当你自己的痛苦
武装你以面对别人的
痛苦。

他走进来
没有摘掉帽子，但若有所思地
擦了擦鞋。桌子
另一头的女士们是木匠
戴着护膝套。屋子
这一头，
是一桌粗野的男子
近坐在一起像在密谋什么
他们的眼角里
相互审视着
对方。狂笑
蔓延开，打断着
简短的笑话。

在吧台上，蜂蜜

瓶子泡在一碗

水里。因为

有蚂蚁。标签上

写着宿醉

安装服务。

迎着柴油味的

风，等

他的行李。默默地

颤抖，张着嘴。

用指关节

揉他的双眼。

琐碎、欺骗、
可笑事物的
壮观化，
模仿模仿的
模仿加剧着
吸尘器的抽力。

我从他们的声音里听出
他们很忙，他们
从我的声音里听出我很忙。
无视多重的
危险。人就是
这么活着。

你是说

大概多早?

她问道。

这儿有一根一端带环的钢丝。

无限的直觉。

另一端,我拧上了一个锥形盖子

底部边缘锋利。

无限总是能在无限的

背景下被直觉到。如果

它不能打开

一个声音,比如我嘴唇间

释放你名字的特别的声音,

那可能涉及到一个腺体

还需要另一种

治疗方案。你能不能

给我沉浸在忧郁里的双眼

撒一把你无限的光幻视呢?

你的句子以铜光般的笑声结尾。

这最后的、现在的阶段，

我的阶段，一个期待的阶段，

反向实现我

这儿的意外，我不受

重视的特权，今天

这个阶段也会达到成熟点

导致体温

略有升高

紧接着喉咙

和下颚发炎

很多红色的淋巴结

肿胀化脓。医生的建议：不要用

手指去拨弄。即使

最好的治疗最终也还是不够有效。

没有失去

他自己的声音

却找到另一个

不合适的

声音。

"如果你想

撒点

土的话，" 牧师

对鳏夫和

他的孩子淡淡地说

但没有

把那句话

说完。

牙齿间

夹着

老鼠般的痛苦

给所有人看。就。

试。试。从。我。这。

拿。走。

他最自然的感觉

是正义感。自我

陶醉的错误。但是

现在则是恐怖。

把真实

吸入现实：那是

毒品的功能。

满地龙葵和羽扇豆

田野斑驳成紫色。

喉头戴红的鸟

在串钱柳花间。

自我的平庸让它更夺目。

狗长嚎着
塞壬的调子。或许
这对夫妇就会到来
让一个个事件
给他们
另一个涵义。就
在她瞳孔脱钩的
刹那，他僵硬了。

蒸发：边境历史

农民，他们是这么叫
　　　　走鹃的，大地的兄弟。十几个
墨西哥人的尸体在沙漠的
　　　　　　日照下变成栗色。
　　　　河边的杨木间，
斑尾鹰尖叫着。从空中
　　　　可以看到，一条废弃跑道的
碎裂痕迹
　　　　　　　覆盖
　　　　有毒的废物和未引爆的弹药。
　　　　周围是紫色和黄色相间的
盛开的花茎：墨西哥龙舌兰。
　　　　　　火山烟囱从贫瘠的平原上
　　　　　　　向上推起。在裸露的
　　　　玄武岩上闪烁，拳头大小的
　　　　　　长石晶体。科曼奇县的
　　　　突袭小径汇合成
一条满是蹄印的通道。

铁丝网上

极乐鸟

令人惊恐的尖叫。一百五十英里

都被监控，白色浮空器

看起来像鲸鱼。山峰间

是黑豹岩盖。两个牛仔

全身赤裸，在蚁丘上吼叫。

雌蝈蝈朝着唧唧叫鸣的雄性

挥动她的前腿鼓膜。细

粒的入侵遍布山上

也渗入漆间山。

他的马痛苦地颤抖着，被一柄长矛击倒在地。

一群冠顶霸鹟在田野上空盘旋。

边境巡逻犬朝着空中马车飞机轮胎

抬起腿来。鞭蛇栅栏

与道路平行。吉娃娃

小道接着阿拉米达小溪。他们叫它

甩马仙人掌。

越战时期的地震探头

埋在私有地里。熔岩石

贴在边上。

歇一歇吧，知更鸟。

人烟稀少。巨型丝兰和束草。

又有什么冒险进入了炎热的下午？只有那些透明蚂蚁。

只有那绝缘的黄粉虫。

路面两侧，测传感器

记录着运动和方向。晚间的

蝉声模糊了树蟋。

有人在粗面岩柱下

赶一千头牛。黄昏里的白尾灰兔

在啃着一只仙人掌果。

黄昏下的逃犯。这些化石层

以小型动物著称。血腥的

明证，暴露

阳光下。我们的历史

任务。无声

尸体的

嚎叫。

鲁思

她丈夫死人一般
躺在椅子里，对着
电视，整天都是
沉默，她自己的想法，
她的听觉，
受创。不会
再好起来了。绝对
没有什么好期待的了，她说
如果不是你，
那是对谁?

她穿着两只一样的

左脚的鞋。没人

相信我没

染发，她

第 n 次

说道。明白了，我

比我母亲

衰老，尽管

在镜子里，我看得到

她的脸，她的深色

小眼睛。

往北五个州，他

在想是什么

引起了

这嗖嗖声

他听到身后

他母亲的

声音：她

倒在

地上，一只手

拿着电话

而另一只

手，她准是

在给肿瘤狗

挠痒，

狗爪

不自觉地

抓着地毯。

绿盒子在床头柜上

眼镜系在红人[1]挂绳上

绿色眼镜盒子里

有一只助听器

没有电池，在床头柜上

眼镜系在红人挂绳上

在绿色的草地里

其中一只喂鸟器下

在后院到处飞着

模糊的、喑哑的鸟

---

1 美国职业棒球队辛辛那提红人。

偶尔喷涕傻笑

或是哽咽 而心电图的

哗哗声很稳定。

鸟喙般坚定的

要做个好人的

决心，现在都

上哪儿去了？

怎么可能是

真的，

我现在

得走了？她忘了

我的名字，却要

我更多的

陪伴。现在

我孑然

一身，我的

母亲又是谁？

所以握着她的手在公园里
散步：那动物般的暖心时刻
我们一坐下她就不记得了。贪婪的
燕八哥停在摇摆着的硬脂笼子上。
她眼里标志式的热情和折磨
混在一起。无所谓
你选什么，疾病
总是赢家。像沉沉的坎肩，
云朵的阴影拖过
地平线上的山峦。或许是我
误读了她的表情。

坠入爱河像跌在人行道上。
醒来好像我是拉响的警报。
惧怕把食物放进我的
嘴里，我的肚子咯咯地叫
像无数只马蛭。所以
没有你，未来的日子会打开，
在你走过的地方扔下蛋黄。
而白色的月见草会疯狂地
起泡，像你快乐的碎片
拒绝抛弃我。诸如此类。
圣坛上的镜子是回忆。你
所经历的现在转到我身上
又在这片大地上存在。一群鹅
在土坑里筛来筛去。呕吐后的
酸涩灼伤了我的喉咙。

发现此刻时间突破了自我

脱离事件的自然顺序，穿越

时势桎梏的空隙

带着迷惑的骑手

进入绵延不断的、轮廓冬雾般模糊的平原。

◆ ◆ ◆

她是如何和安眠药作斗争，陪我从海滩开车回来，一直聊着天，说着话或是听我说：声音让人安心，即使是她现在上了药后不断重复的含糊也听起来像低低的鸟鸣，暮色中盲目的问询——有人在吗？——她活着的证明，她就在这儿，在我旁边的座位上系着安全带，她克服了药效，这可恶的障碍历程，我给她注射了嗜睡感，以便我今晚能开四小时的车送她回家，能集中注意力开车，能挽救我加班说话、花粉过敏肿胀、多痰发炎的嗓子，能避免重复的问题，她挣扎于生活的碎片和熟悉的名字从脸和情感上分离，她的丈夫、孙儿的昵名，一种空白的语言，我左手放在方向盘上开车，另一只手抚摸她手上松垮的皮肤，感觉到她手掌上紧缩的腱膜，筋膜带让她的手指向前弯曲，当我觉得她终于睡着了的时候，她仰起的脸来了精神，此时我们正在穿过印度河湾，她以前经常和我父亲在这儿，在他们的格帝威游艇上钓比目鱼，游艇的单舷外引擎开始泵转，他们带着惊愕在一片蓝烟中提前数小时就冲入贝瑟尼运河，驶过一个个浮标——红色方向正确——穿过阿萨女子湾，经过鱼叉汉娜海鲜餐厅，驶入打着哈欠的大西洋——这时我想把我的手收回，她却抓得更紧，眼睛没睁开，或者是反射，坚持着和我一起醒着的意愿，她的儿子，她认得他，她现在在她半睡、麻醉疲劳的状态下，在药力挥发的作用下，感谢他，是我骗她把药吞下的，因为希望这次车行对她来说更容易些，坐我旁边，抓紧。

◆ ◆ ◆

没穿衬衣也没穿裤子，她坐在床边，把手伸到后背去解文胸。我帮她站起来，脱下她的内裤，她痛苦地倒向一边，尽管没有任何抱怨。

她上厕所的方式是在我们帮她穿上睡衣前赤身裸体地上。她既不害羞也不为自己的身体感到自豪。即使小的时候，我就明白她认为身体是一种工具。无论我和姐妹们遭受过怎样的心理创伤，我们对身体不会感到不自然，不会对裸体感到不好意思。

在我面前，我的母亲看起来比穿着衣服的时候更圆润，但当她蹒跚着走向卫生间，伸手够把手的时候，她却是一幕斑斑点点的生死剧，她的后臀坍塌成了一层层疙瘩，椎体成形术留下的伤疤消失在了一片褐黄斑中，她的腰间满是下垂的肉。

回忆：在拉巴斯，谈到未来的时候，艾马拉[1] 老者会在肩膀上面向后挥手。说到过去，他们会做向前推动的手势。艾马拉语里，眼、前和视线意味着过去，而未来意味着身后或后背。在我母亲的身体里，她的前身是过去，而她的后背是未来。

---

1 南美洲安第斯及阿尔蒂普拉诺地区的土著民族。

她坐着，我绑住她脚踝上的睡裤，先这一边再那一边，她以复杂的慢动作前倾站起来时，我把她的裤子拉上。另一个世界受伤的仙鹤。

◆ ◆ ◆

重新专注地听每一次重复，就像那是第一次，忘记你之前听到过，她说的话是她最早说的或是最后说的，她重复不仅因为她忘记了也是因为她要把话记住。进入与她告别的节奏，标记、享受每一个周期，以此来打开熟悉的旧爱里的另一种爱，无尽的接受，毫无条件，类似于一位母亲对她孩子的感情。

◆ ◆ ◆

想要却不能。我不能死，她说，眉毛
收紧了，详说重点。病人监护仪
鸣叫着，像在永恒黑夜里的
电子蟋蟀。或是一种顺从的智能。红色
标记很清晰。今天早上卡琳给你涂口红了吗？
氧气罐上的阀门转了九十度。我们
在日常面包连锁店买了晚餐。医院的
窗外，星星在斑节虾星云的
紫外线照射下闪动着。而你是。什么？
是一只蜂鸟，她说。我的天，真心的，
请让她快好起来吧。尽管我早已
蒙受你的恩惠。

水边域

入 口

不管这黑色是不是内核式的——这儿是浮游植物的，那儿是有机
盘曲的——或仅仅是这些精致球形的背景：散发莹莹的光，空灵、
带着条纹状的叶脉，没有被剥下的迹象。

形状像组织一样是白色的吗？是纱布？
不，它们是透明的、白色的。
是膜状的吗？
是牛奶的质地。
那它们相互缠绕的垂直推力呢？
显示在那影响下，它们合并了。

我们肺深处的
长叹。四肢的长度
在发皱的床单上
悬而未决：
所以爱情再次萌芽，
再次颤抖
在大地之烟上。

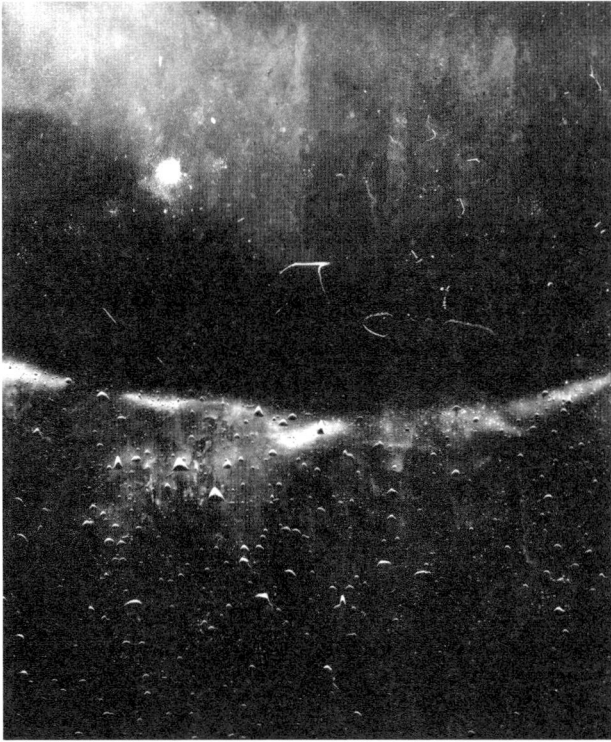

出口

成群的投射小绒球（泡腾般）在嘴唇上升起，拉成沮丧的龇牙咧嘴，飘荡，消失在斑驳的后壁上。

这样的光，如象牙刨刀般耀眼。多节小花在曲线上放射般地撞击弹回，曲线放大距离，距离压迫前景。这样的即兴创作是自然生发的吗？又能与谁分享？

致命烈焰：我们
在彩通的黑上投下
双重阴影。我火蜥蜴的
渴望在你夜的峡谷间
停滞不前。
直到你
从无形的峭壁上
向后退步，而我则是
幽灵般颤动的一堆废物。

入口

他们航行过泊在夜里的白色平顶山上，撞上乳白色的钟乳。彩纹玛瑙。没有明显的光源。

突然感到这般的毫无意义，但还能再要求什么呢？觉察到还没有堕落成习惯？要是相对我们所谓的"觉察"，另一种觉察力所要求的不能实现呢？转身的瞬间，脑中留有的画面摧毁了才落入视线的事物。

我的左旋异构体[1]
在光感上是活跃、情色的。
扫过仿浮游物和你
审视的一瞥：缠绕着
秸秆，我们空空地抵着墙：
象形文字的漂流物
混在一堆蝌蚪里。

---

1 能使平面偏振光向左旋转的光线异构体。

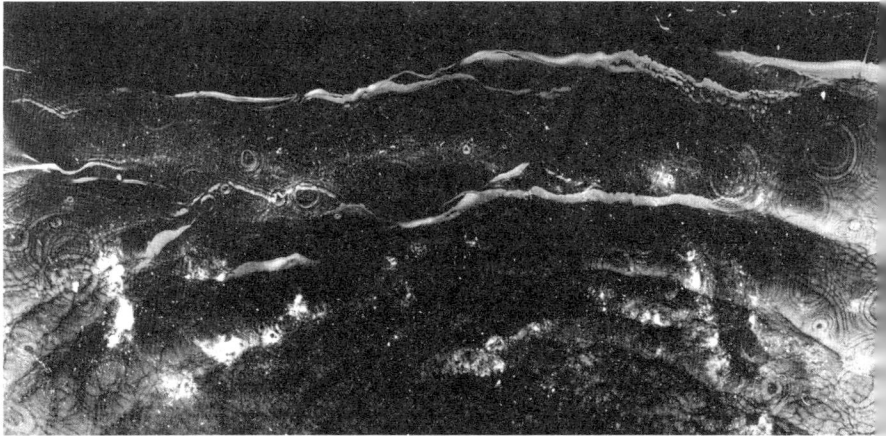

出口

树干、水圈、藤壶伤疤，放射状的涟漪碰撞，打皱皮肤，什么上
的皮肤？渐开线区间从拉长石的光泽里浮起，一片波浪阴影满目
疮痍，打亮的边缘吐着蒸汽。

如果美洲狮能说话，那又有谁不能理解她呢？路上，黄夹克和彩
绘女们闪着光，渗水打暗了黏土，滑面透光。神圣的石头。

塞壬的声音
围绕我们
在淤积的
区域，同时
闪电勾勒出
夜的褶皱。接着
是刺痛：我
坍塌了，你
消失了。只有
我的眼睛。眼睛。放大。

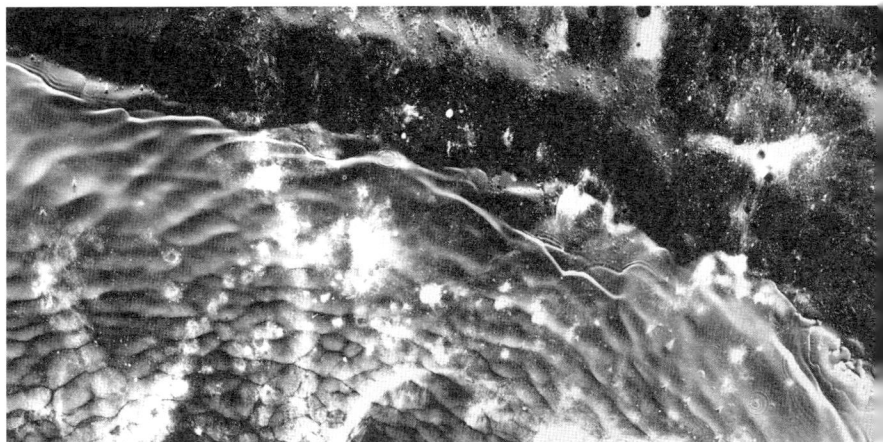

入口

涂上太阳的热烈，碳化的溶解。液体零界点上呈颗粒状。深色的科迪勒拉山边，海岸线上打着泡沫。

是什么经历证实了这个画面？是以厘米还是英里来衡量？还是衡量的表述要靠某种隐喻？假设确实有这样一个地方。但要是这样的"地方"从未存在，而永远只是交换的方式，像数月后要付的丧葬费？

神经行为
靠近你呼吸的
动量零界点，我们
聚积的焚烧，未
被打烂的绽放：颠倒
水坑。正是我们
湿漉漉的肉体
把我们从焦灼的
天使报喜中
拯救出来。

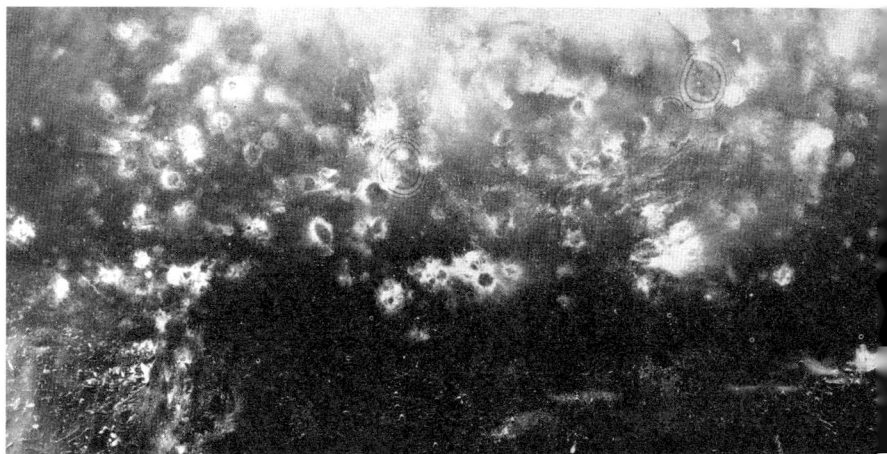

出 口

成群的磷光，气态群。呼吸起伏燃成无形的外皮。在这火山凝灰岩上，亲密开始。在这里坚持。

尽管我们对如何观察没有标准，也不确定我们观察到的是什么，我们被打入了兴奋状态。就像进入了一种新的疼痛状态。但冷静的描述又曾带来过什么呢？

你重创的留痕
挤满我大脑的
树脂。变格，
焦点上的痉挛。当你的
眼皮释放张力，
夜间的生物群，
脊椎的
和膜状的，都涌进
我的梦里。在远处，
你现在能看到我
短暂地在这幻象里
徘徊，承受
痛苦的漩涡吗？

外两首

周年纪念

不，别让它知道，永远，
永远不要让我的伤口
知道，

我埋下忧郁的幼虫
跟随你。把自己

像黄昏一般
收拢在你黑色郁金香的乳头。（郁金香，郁金香）。

整整七天，我们锁上门
用鸟类的血搓洗着房间。

片刻间
你的喉咙玫瑰般

在你绚烂的锁骨间升起 （玫瑰，玫瑰），
我们仅有的对手只是音乐，

骨白色的钢琴。

光没有暗下来，

反而深深地收缩。

裸露地看。

颤抖。

一片空地

你要去哪儿？风尘仆仆的。你从哪儿来？
突兀无味的乱石堆，一片贫瘠的王国。
一只手掌般大的狼蛛在破瓦砾边包裹着土。

穿过这里的不是长着牙就是带着刺，穿上了这片土地的颜色。
边缘浅黄色的阴影。
你要去哪儿？风尘仆仆的。你从哪儿来？

破败工棚边担架上装满了土块。
烧灼的地形，这是什么意思？
向前一步，他和我们在一起。后退一步，另一个空间收留他。

时代感松了，散了。
每个人都认为是另一个像地平线般后退。
他皮肤下神奇的笼子清晰可见。

他的双眼说，我不能抛弃我。
笛子吹奏着一个音符。一张脸。
露天下的正午，男人们在强光下萎缩。

石头说，我可以被解读，但你不可以。

抛光的空气，矿物般，一层薄薄的云母。

照片上的土墩，眼睛里的虹膜。

烧灼的地形，这是什么意思？

拯救石头中万物的颜色万物中石头的颜色。

她的双眼说，我可以被解读，但你不可以。

就好像大地抛弃了自己。

被赤裸的山丘大雨般冲刷，土地在风中变成沙粒。

向前一步，我们和它们在一起。后退一步，另一个空间收留我们。

他说，别拣石头，因为石头属于死去的人。

边缘浅黄色的阴影。

距离如马毛石膏般平坦，所有的深度被挤平了。

黑色的尾矿堆。

他和我们的双眼之间空无一物，连邀请都没有。

每块石头都带着它的死刑来到这个有生的世界。

飞蛆吃着红蚂蚁的脑子。

时代感松了，散了。

光在空中断了。

男人的阴影和树枝的阴影有着相同的质地。

凝住神，一片余晖。

所有的深度被挤平了，距离如马毛石膏般平坦 。

眼睛里的虹膜，照片上的土墩。

石头说，别把他拣起来，因为死去的人属于石头。

在破瓦砾边包裹着土，一只手掌般大的狼蛛。

男人的阴影和树枝的阴影有着相同的质地。

穿过这里的不是长着牙就是带着刺，穿上了这片土地的颜色。

空气被抛了光，几近于矿物。

相伴于弗罗斯特·甘德的《相伴》

（美）查尔斯·阿尔铁里[1]

李栋　译

1　查尔斯·阿尔铁里（Charles Altieri），美国著名文学批评家，加州
大学伯克利分校英语系主任。

键盘敲入标题的时候，我意识到这种祈使式的"相伴"不只是对读者发出的邀请，也对作者提出了强烈的要求。就对读者的邀请而言，我只想说这个标题出色地阐释了诗歌如何能够提供与别的写作方式截然不同的生命体验。邀请读者参与到作品中来，对甘德一书尤为合适，因为他需要通过一种独特的话语方式来建立与世界的关系，并以此来弥补失去他深爱的妻子 C. D. 莱特的痛苦。

　　就对作者提出的要求而言，我有几点要说。甘德在之前相关的访谈中谈到丧妻之痛促成了这本书。我想强调他是如何通过此书的写作以求得恢复。此书没有刻意抹去失去妻子带来的痛苦，而是试图从根本上建立一种对生命更全面的认识。恢复取决于甘德和我们能否充分意识到：其实，他的标题回应了亡妻诗集里留给他的同样的"相伴"二字，并唤起了期间他所经历的转变。相应地，甘德在《招魂》一诗结尾处开始确立他生命中要改变的事物，在散文、杂文中他也常常引用诗集里这绝妙的第二首：

　　这时我的悲音跳出了语言。

　　像一群漂流的蜜蜂。

这时接着重重的沉默。

我被蜜蜂击晕，失去意识。

这时也没有我的出路。

这时我半浑半噩地活着，梦见我还醒着，

……

这时她的声音固定在了蒸气色的背景上。

这时沙丘鹤的尾羽亮了。

……

这时我幻想一个比人生更真实的空间。

这时至少还有某种可能。

某种……我不相信的可能。

这首诗特别运用了语法的效应来加强其张力。重复"这时"使此诗因亡妻而想抓住"重重的沉默"的瞬间又最终自我挫败的努力得以戏剧化。努力之所以自我挫败是因为，假设努力成功的话，他将深陷对前世所失去事物的认识中。这种失落的核心在于，努力将自我意识埋藏在极度悲痛和诗人的"我"之间不可承受的张力之中。而这个"我"又无法抗拒自我转变的意识，并害怕这种意识会营造出另一种现实。这种情形几乎发生了，不过拥有地质学位的诗人没能满足于"一个比人生更真实的空间"，而这句话本身就是带着讽刺和苦涩的一语双关："空间"（realm）和"真实"（real）之间令人不安的关联定义了问题所在。诗歌的精确指代也无法实现再次和他妻子在一起。也就是说，必须要有别样的沉默、别样的方式让诗里的蜜蜂能唤醒标题所追寻的存在方式。

这里"相伴"（be with）使用的分词形式说明我们知道祈使人和介词的宾语。我们还知道这种特殊性不能唤起他所需要的信仰形式。相反，对他妻子特殊品质回归的希望和不可能性带来了更多的痛和羞耻，而不是愉悦和可再生的活力。亡妻回归的不可能性更清楚表明书名为何无法填补语法的空白。"相伴"祈使式两头都是开放的，旨在确立别样思考的重要性：诗进入的世界必须依靠语法来表明诗歌创造的空间可以用来探索实践推理之外的想象领域。打开新的想象领域甚至可能提供对隐约闪现在语言下的现实的新认识。这些领域或许也为"相伴"的祈使式提供了源头以及对什么能补足"相伴"提供了新认识。这一补足甚至会把我们的注意力从宾语转移到情态限定词上，因为这些诗并不需要太多的关注对象，而是新的态度和别致的语气使想象力能更好地表达所承受的痛苦：

发现此刻时间突破了自我

脱离事件的自然顺序，穿越

时势桎梏的空隙

带着迷惑的骑手

　　　　　进入绵延不断的、轮廓冬雾般模糊的平原。

更笼统地讲，标题的不确定性必须被视为强加了至少一种明确的自我意识。除了像《鲁思》一诗中被压抑的记忆外，这本诗集不关注特定场景或是戏剧性的情节。没有戏剧性的情节反而为甘德所需要的重要事物提供了舞台。他委婉地宣布此书关注人的命运以及对建立可靠的、值得信赖的关系的需求，并以此来补偿他的痛苦，但又不假装这些能抹去丧妻之痛。甘德需要另一种爱的对象，这个对象应该把丧妻之痛作为根本的条件——不仅是对逝去妻子的回忆，还包括与哀悼不可分割的自卑自弃所唤起的记忆——从而使建立新的联系成为可能。这本诗集必须展示失去深爱之人的悲伤是如何与深深不满于失去机会成为爱能创造的人密不可分。为了阐明对命运—— 而不是事件本身——的认识，这本诗集必须建构起特定情况下的同理心与对继续生活下去的新认识的差异性。

各种揭开甘德书名奥秘的方法让我能够证明为什么我认为这是当代重要的文本。它已超越了一个极度真挚、聪颖的人是如何处理失去爱人的痛苦而又不放弃爱的方式。（因为也有写他儿子和他母亲日渐衰老的诗，我得把爱变成复数。）我们首先必须认识到赞扬（或主张）对复杂生态关系认识的写作与说明生态意识对日常生活中价值取向重要性的写作存在着极大的不同。我是在理查德·鲍尔斯（Richard Powers）的惊人作品《树语者》（与甘德同一年获普利策奖）这本从树的角度想象人的生命的书里看到了这种差异。与人类相比，树木有着截然不同、更为宽广的时间意识。它们对环境中的各类关系的处理比大多数人更复杂和仁慈。在用树木的寿命所衡量的历史框架下，鲍尔斯把人类的灾难作为相对微小的事实来处理，所以多的是同情而不是怜悯。

甘德与鲍尔斯大为不同：鲍尔斯重点讲人类努力考虑全局从而使树木能够成为地球生命的典范；而作为地理学家的甘德对密切关注生物处理与同类的亲密关系所产生的意识状态更感兴趣。鲍尔斯似乎要一种新伦理；而甘德想要为如敬畏、随性的甘心屈从等宗教状态提供新的基础。[1]

我想详细阐述甘德关于生态价值主张的三种基本方式，以及由此诗集的最根本问题——"如果不是并置，她问道，那什么是联系的桥梁？"——所生发出的一种自我意识的独特模式。什么样的视角可以将悲伤视为一种认知工具，并用以见证对环境的密切关注是如何能够阐明评估经验的新模式的。首先，甘德生态意识最重要的方面在于一贯坚持宗教理想——不仅是所产生的宗教崇拜，也是所激发的自我意识的特定状态。甘德不拒绝科学，但他也深知关于爱和失去的问题所需要的思考模式抵制了科学对事

1　甘德关于生态的写作，请参见他和澳大利亚诗人约翰·金塞拉（John Kinsella）2012 年在美国爱荷华大学出版社出版的《红尾鸲（Redstart）》一书。

物运作方式所做出的积极、正面的回答："但冷静的描述又曾带来过什么呢？" 甘德致力于用科学在充满活力的微环境中绘制出复杂、亲密状态的图像。而这种活力取决于接受场景内的全部——常常是仅仅由一个遥远、广阔视野贯穿起来的挣扎的时时刻刻。甘德还运用地质学的词汇坚持抵抗多愁善感所掩饰的痛苦。设想在各个层面都几乎令人震惊的以下这个例子，甘德用跨行的形式来结束一段想象和他妻子莱特的对话：

［如果］它不能打开

一个声音，比如我嘴唇间

释放你名字的特别的声音，

那可能涉及到一个腺体

还需要另一种

治疗方案。你能不能

给我沉浸在忧郁里的双眼

撒一把你无限的光幻视呢？

这种用法提醒我们，在自然过程中总有与我们人类心理状态的类比，而我们自我沉溺，认为这些状态仅限于我们的生命形式。

甘德致力于调和科学与宗教信仰的努力在他的诗《第一首叙事诗：花环》里首次获得了极为正面的表达：花环让圣十字若望承受痛苦。我认为这首诗由三部分组成。第一部分是五个诗节赞美"道"赋予生命以形式。我觉得下面的五个诗节，也就是第二部分，引出了圣神。第三部分：三位一体认识到圣子的话语是如何准确反映了圣父的绝对权威，因此，圣神必须被这种反映所唤起的爱充溢：

爱于人被爱于   人如此类推
而缠绕他们的爱   归一

总结两个   声音一个被爱
两人之中   每个个体间

同一幸福   使其成为同一情人
没有坦白的光   辉——灿烂

两人聚于一体   个体拥有
个体于爱中   道的全部

其每一生命   缠绕于人
理解之外   无法打开的结

甘德的留白将孤立的声音变成了复杂的隐喻状态：活彼此的命，死彼此的死。但他还是依赖隐喻，也就是说一种信念：他必须以最具体的方式来转变。因此，他加了三行尾曲让不同诗行的结合展示出异于其生发过程的最后一种状态：

如此炽烈的爱   把两人缠绕

两人拥有同一声音　　　　　　　世界的全部

爱愈是同一　　　　　　　　　　就愈有爱

　　或许有范例说明爱人的结合如何建立了一种超越他们身体最终分离的状态。所面临的挑战是把圣人的远见看成权威的具体实现，为此，我们现在必须找到新的语言和新的表现方式。在这种情况下，表现方式涉及语言的各方面如何相互嵌入，以此来表现什么持续存在于躯体之外。这种嵌入部分表现为分离读者极力想放在一起的词组，并通过同样的方式来修补这些分离："道"最终会唤起爱的觉醒，表达圣神的存在。这里的留白不仅生发了对差异的意识，也不断要求读者去演示语言如何展开，如何在孤立的词语间产生复杂的融合。语言的这种展开部分表现为把隐喻吸收拉回到能想象到的最具体、质朴的语言。最终，找到鲜活的"道的全部"也就重塑了"世界的全部"。

　　这首诗试图将其对声音的关注和词语间不断产生的沉默联系起来。这让我们关注到第二种更为具体的将精神力量引入生态关系的方式。《相伴》不断探索沉默如何提供充满交流可能性的空间——比如，《招魂》一诗的双行体以及《第一首叙事诗：花环》和其他诗的留白。这些做法延续了甘德对道的神学兴趣。在这本集子里，我们能看到这些表达丰富的沉默并不需要神学的约束。相反，在欣赏这种诗歌最具体的方面，我们能找到相应的神学结构。这本书最重要的基石就是 C. D. 莱特的字面意义上的沉默。然而，围绕在诗人甘德周围的一切似乎都有很多话要说，诗人也常提到自己的失败：没能找到恰当的词，没能把词语排成合适的结构来赞美他们两人之间的爱。这种赞美需要以超验状态类似宗教式的欣赏作为背景。所以甘德不得不问，是否有世俗沉默方式能提供达到先验的类似途径。一个答案是：诗歌本身通过各种留白来增强话语的抒情力量，从而使沉默也能开口说话。要找到"相伴"一词祈使式的基础以及缺失的宾语，那就得依赖《第一首叙事诗：花环》和《情理》中展现的沉默所提供的线索。

甘德把着墨最深的沉默留给了最后一组诗《水边域》。在这组诗里，甘德巧妙实现了他最心向往之的诗学方向，即诗歌和摄影如何结合：摄影把具体瞬间的沉默流动性拉出时间的维度，引入思考的空间，对此，诗歌可以如何处理？与摄影的联系是此诗集中第三种也是最有力的方式：让意识扎根于具体物像，从而打开一种他与亡妻在精神上可行的、持续的关系。这里，相辅的艺术只能是写实性的摄影，或至少是建立在事实基础上的摄影作品，因为沉默很现实地存在于世上，诗人必须相应地发声。摄影作品结合了科学工具来帮助我们通过诗人的眼光看到可能带来的本体论意义。世俗的词面对世俗的世界，而其间融合的想象力将为"相伴"为何是祈使式提供答案。

"水边域"是指海岸线上阳光充足、能供给植物生命的部分。甘德回应了摄影师迈克尔·弗洛曼（Michael Flomen）的六幅摄影作品。这些作品表现了水流是如何影响不同水边域周围的光线。甘德这组诗中，三首以《入口》命名，三首以《出口》命名，最后一首《出口》诗试图教我们如何摆脱念念不忘的人和事。每首回应诗都包括三个部分：第一部分是对图片信息的散文化描述，第二部分是对所处情境在情感上的诗文相结合的表达，第三部分是从诗学和隐喻角度出发，现实场景到说话人扣问存在意义空间的极度延伸。在这儿，我想处理第一首《入口》和最后一首《出口》。

第一幅摄影作品描绘了色调和阴影间无法定位的奇妙流动，不同形体错综复杂地相互渗透，光影斑驳间突显斑点运动作用于所处的结构并使之充满生机。

文本如下：

不管这黑色是不是内核式的——这儿是浮游植物的，那儿是有机盘曲的——或仅仅是这些精致球形的背景：散发莹莹的光，空灵、带着条纹状的叶脉，没有被剥下的迹象。

形状像组织一样是白色的吗？是纱布？

不，它们是透明的、白色的。

是膜状的吗?

是牛奶的质地。

那它们相互缠绕的垂直推力呢?

显示在那影响下,它们合并了。

我们肺深处的

长叹。四肢的长度

在发皱的床单上

悬而未决:

所以爱情再次萌芽,

再次颤抖

在大地之烟上。

这是什么入口,哪里的入口?我认为入口是指尊重作品的沉默及其相关的情感可能性的表达方式。最为引人注目的是散文部分,技术上的精确性展示了变向思维能力是如何看穿表象变化的。这种思维提供了三种思考方式的入口,或者说"空灵、带着条纹状的叶脉,没有被剥下"到从属的地位。每种思考方式都有独特的角色要扮演。整体而言,这组诗摆脱了前面的诗里单一关注无法走出回忆和耻辱的自我意识,从而提供了另一种有力的可能性。这种可能性揭示了一种新方式来迫使诗集里的痛苦进入一种更为具体的空间,由此而产生的视野把极度的特殊性与一种抽象、不具人情味的、能够适应物质元素复杂关系的话语模式结合起来。

画面的所有细节都不能让人联想到任何一处具体场所：这些细节提供了可完全吸收智力和关怀的模式，摈弃了让关怀岌岌可危的、问题重重的人为情境。

这样的思考是不可能引出人性关系的全景的，也不可能替代莱特和甘德曾一起经历的事物。然而，这里有一种与错综复杂的物质世界相关联的补偿性的密度，能打开"颤抖／在大地之烟上"这样的隐喻，打开经历的新维度。这些颤抖，这些多维度激烈运动和微妙关系的视觉呈现让"爱情再次萌芽"——不是在通俗剧中，我们必须担心自我需求使然的夸大，而是诠释因内容的多形式而激动得颤抖。最让我惊异的是我本人如何通过文本看到情色默默展开，文本带我们领略这首诗是如何诠释这个情境并与情色多层面结合的。

但我们不可能永远停留在这些图片带我们进入的空间，一定还要有出口——作者因需求驱动的想象力，这本诗集也不会放弃促生它的痛苦。出口也是一种许可，以此来接受未来将回忆重新投入到现实的种种可能。摄影作品脱离语言桎梏的这种基本动力可以让我们看到，投入到现实的可能性包括了想象情色的新方式。新方式并不否认回忆不能抹去的事物，而是起到了补充的作用。这一组诗可能更接近《第一首叙事诗：花环》所想象的情爱之事。

最后这首诗所附带的摄影照片看起来像海浪撞击岩石后，岩石吐出微生物，漂浮在画面上方，寻求释放。

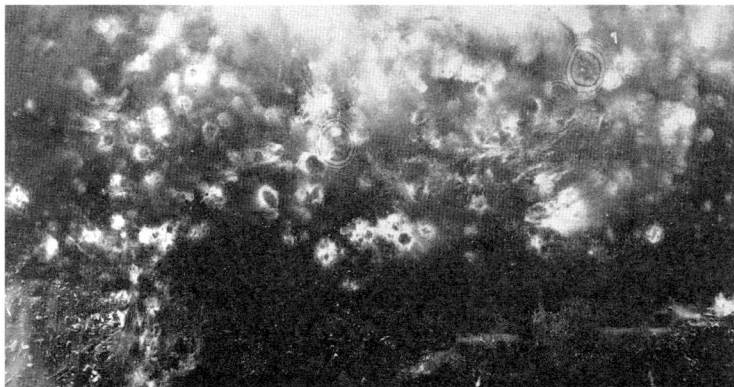

　　我们又能如何不运用隐喻来找到从记录痛苦失败纯粹描述的
职责中释放想象力的可能？

　　成群的磷光，气态群。呼吸起伏燃成无形的外皮。在这火山
凝灰岩上，亲密开始。在这里坚持。

　　尽管我们对如何观察没有标准，也不确定我们观察到的是什
么，我们被打入了兴奋状态。就像进入了一种新的疼痛状态。但
冷静的描述又曾带来过什么呢？

　　你重创的留痕
　　挤满我大脑的
　　树脂。变格，
　　焦点上的痉挛。当你的
　　眼皮释放张力，

夜间的生物群，

脊椎的

和膜状的，都涌进

我的梦里。在远处，

你现在能看到我

短暂地在这幻象里

徘徊，承受

痛苦的漩涡吗？

这里，生命更迭的希望让人感觉第二人称的使用恰到好处。如果不这样，又如何能记录下一个全新视角下大脑对生命本能的反应呢？图片所表现的灵敏的大脑依赖于从岩石到光的运动，也就是从阴影到波浪撞击释放多种微生物的自由。这强大的存在感决定了第二人称特别指代C. D. 莱特，她现在已与原动力不可分了。多数诗人就此事件作诗会依赖标准的抒情形式，但甘德却以语言科学为基础的复杂又有力的结构来结尾。幻影般的对峙似乎指代了图片中原动力与被释放的"夜间的生物群"的结合。之后，这种对峙转化为"承受／痛苦的漩涡"。漩涡的产生来自于睡眠上燃料燃烧生成熊熊的火山，然后转化为平静旋转的蓝线。

再没有比这更奇异而合适的形而上的隐喻了。放下悲伤的第一阶段所产生的强烈情绪，也就是认同了悲伤标志着痛苦与解脱、激情与进入纯粹形式的入口共同存在。这与从皮肤到绞合线的复杂转变相平行。转变在第二首诗《出口》中达到了极致：一根绷紧的丝线最终从一个曲面被绕开。细腻的丝线将已成为"绞合线"

的"皮肤"化成"拉长石的光泽"。拉长石是一种极富灵性的色彩斑斓的矿物石，能增强物质与灵异界的联系。最后这首《出口》诗对此做了补充，其不仅与永恒平衡关系的内在细节相关联，也为关照和关怀提供了结构。舞动的火与那一片水域融合于心，我们因此可以看到打开非人类世界的当务之急：一种安静却又炽烈，对万物更为博大的爱；这种爱为自我定义提供了客观细致的框架，慰藉感也由此扩展成了积极的同情心。

一本与爱、生命、死亡相对称的诗集

西川

已经有些年头了，我一直这样认为：20 世纪下半叶以来，世界上最好的诗歌出自北美、拉美、东欧，现在中国诗人们正在向这个阵线努力靠近。——当然这是就整体而言，不是说在其他地区、其他语言里没有孤立存在的重要诗人。

　　中国普通的诗歌读者们无不熟悉 19 世纪的美国大诗人瓦尔特·惠特曼，而专业一些的诗歌读者们读美国现代诗歌也已经有好几代人了。我们中间的某些人几乎像美国专业诗歌读者一样熟悉埃兹拉·庞德、T. S. 艾略特、华莱士·史蒂文斯、威廉·卡洛斯·威廉斯、罗伯特·弗罗斯特、伊丽莎白·毕肖普、罗伯特·罗威尔、西尔维娅·普拉斯、安妮·塞克斯顿、艾伦·金斯伯格、盖瑞·斯奈德、W. S. 默温、查尔斯·奥尔森、查尔斯·布考斯基等等。20 世纪上半叶的美国诗歌（也加上 1950—1960 年代的垮掉派、自白派、黑山派），其多样性、开放性、丰富性、实验性有目共睹。这在世界现代诗歌风景中相当醒目。造就此一风景的，除了美国文学发展的内在逻辑，可能也与美国诗人们自觉并且积极地接受来自不同地域，尤其是古代东亚和拉美诗歌的影响分不开。近二十多年来，美国当代诗歌的面目也向我们慢慢呈现。艾略特·温伯格（Eliot Weinberger）编选的《1950 年后的美国诗歌：革新者和局外人》一书，早在 2003 年就由诗人马永波翻译，由河北教育出版社出版了，其中又收录了更多也更晚近的美国诗人的作品。从中我们可以感到，其创造活力、革新精神一以贯之。

2005 年 7 月，诗人翟永明在成都艺术双年展期间曾试图组织"世纪城·首届成都国际诗歌节"。那次活动由于种种原因，最终没能搞成，但她所邀请的外国诗人们——其中包括我以前在美国就认识的艾略特·温伯格和弗罗斯特·甘德——却来到了成都。弗罗斯特还在成都丢了钱包。记得在成都我们暂住的酒店，有一回艾略特提起他编选的《1950 年后的美国诗歌》的中译本，为该书未获版权授予便出版略显不快，同时又为书中没有收入弗罗斯特的作品而向坐在旁边的他表示歉意。弗罗斯特没有表现出任何不快的样子。那时他作为美国诗坛的后起之秀正快速崛起。

弗罗斯特再次来华是在 2006 年 9 月，参加由中坤集团组织的帕米尔诗歌之旅。那一次他是和妻子 C. D. 莱特（C. D. Wright）一起来的。C. D. 是当代美国的杰出诗人，获得过诸多重要奖项，其中包括 2009 年加拿大的格里芬诗歌大奖（Griffin Poetry Prize），赢得了不同国家诗人们的尊敬。那一次新疆帕米尔之行，他们两人都很愉快。弗罗斯特送给我一本在中国非正式出版的《弗罗斯特·甘德诗选》，中英文对照。中文译者为黄运特、姜泰强、周瓒、朴韵、老哈、蔚群等。感觉弗罗斯特也加入了中国诗人们的民间出版。那是甘德诗第一次成规模地出现在中国诗歌读者面前，尽管这个读者的范围很小。

弗罗斯特·甘德的诗歌魔力满满：从题材上讲，它们有一种纪实性，但其下笔处往往出人意料。其诗歌在形式方面的实验性很强，语言过处，生活获得哲学的打开甚至发明。这样一种富于洞察力的诗歌所展现出的是一种深层次的美，它打动你时，声音不大，但你却被深深地打动，且觉得余音不绝。弗罗斯特的几乎每一行诗都是开花，有时是爆破，但你不知道他后面的诗行又会生出怎样的奇效，故而会有所期待。他的诗歌、他的文学（他也是实验小说作者）、他丰富的感觉和高智力令人信赖。后来我了解到，弗罗斯特早年学的是地质学。其诗歌语言的密实、结实与复杂可能包含了某种诗歌地质学因素：想想那些土壤和岩石、那些缝隙与暗道、那些松软和坚硬、那些流动与沸腾、那些变化和不变。2011 年弗罗斯特出版过一本糅合诗歌、散文和摄影的作品集《来自世界的核心样本》（*Core Samples from the World*）。本书第 1 章记录的是 2006 年他与 C. D. 的新疆帕米尔诗歌之旅。在第 4 章的开头，他有一首诗是写给我的，名为《世界地图》。我把这首诗翻译成了中文，收在我的《重新注册》译诗集中。翻译那首诗时，我切身感受到，弗罗斯特的语言虽然复杂、绵密，但这一切表面看起来又是干净、利索。他高超的语言技艺既是对译者的考验，也是对读者的恩赏。如果我没记错的话，这本书曾经入围普利策奖。

美国当代诗人中既有垮掉派那一路的写法——口语、即兴、日常，甚至疯狂，这其中不乏有诗人热爱东方文化，修悟禅道——当然也有弗罗斯特这一路的写法——这两种写法曾经截然不同，而现在它们会在不同的诗人那里形成不同的合流。弗罗斯特这一路写法的美国谱系，至少包括了庞德传统（历史视野、智力）、史蒂文斯传统（哲思、形式感），外加奥尔森传统（黑山派、形式实验），或者还要加上纽约派。弗罗斯特本人也是现当代拉美西班牙语诗歌积极的译者。2017年9月在阿根廷的罗莎里奥，我问前来参加诗歌节活动的拉美诗人们都读谁，得到的回答是，他们读得最多的是美国诗人。我提到弗罗斯特·甘德的名字，他们都知道。于此可见他在拉美的影响力。至于他本人的创作具体受到哪些拉美诗人、作家的影响，我一时半会儿就说不清楚了。弗罗斯特热情、敏锐、善良。他的文学、文化、历史、政治关怀是世界性的。2011年秋天，因美国铜峡出版社（Copper Canyon）出版了由王清平编选、李春琳（Sylvia Li-chun Lin）、葛浩文（Howard Goldblatt）任译文编辑的《推开窗：中国当代诗歌》（*Push Open the Window: Contemporary Poetry from China*），我和女诗人周瓒受邀一起赴美国做巡回朗诵。在纽约曼哈顿92街Y举办的李立扬（Li-young Lee）、陈美玲（Marilyn Chin）、周瓒和我的朗诵会开始之前，弗罗斯特就诗歌翻译、美国华裔诗人和中国当代诗歌做了长篇的介绍性发言。看得出来，他关心世界上每一个角落的生活、历史与写作。在美国，在拉美，在印度，在日本，在东欧，诗人们受益于弗罗斯特的写作。他的写作铺开的是一张精神性的世界地图，但他从来不曾停留于世界与生活的表面。2007年，我在纽约大学东亚系任教期间曾受邀去耶鲁大学做过一个朗诵或者讲座——记不清了。耶鲁大学有几位诗人组织了一个定期交流的诗歌活动。参加这个活动的诗人们写一种叫做"困难诗"（difficult poetry）的诗。他们瞧不上简易的写作，注重哲思，讲究形式语言。他们都与弗罗斯特·甘德保持着良好的文学和智力关系，并且认定他是一位重要的诗人。

那一年在纽约，我也曾去位于罗德岛普罗维登斯市的布朗大学拜访在那里执教的弗罗斯特和他的妻子、同样是布朗大学写作教授的 C. D. 莱特。他们都是强有力的诗人，而在生活中，他们又是格外谦和的一对儿。C. D. 肤色苍白、体质略弱、仪态文雅，但内心却广大而坚定。

她和弗罗斯特一样，随时准备帮助别人。此前我曾把我的几首长诗的英译文寄给他们。C. D. 把我推荐给了铜峡出版社。C. D. 建议，由她和弗罗斯特帮助润色那份译文。尽管我的英文诗集《蚊子志》（由另一位朋友柯夏智 Lucas Klein 翻译）最终由纽约的新方向（New Directions）出版社出版，但 C. D. 和弗罗斯特对我的友善，我至今铭记在心。我在他们身上看到了高尚，或者用一个我一般会避开的说法：人性的光芒。新方向 2012 年出版《蚊子志》时，是 C. D. 帮我写的推荐语［此外还有盖瑞·斯奈德和瑞克·西蒙森（Rick Simonson）］。

那一天在普罗维登斯，弗罗斯特开车，我坐副驾，C. D. 坐后排，我们去吃饭。阳光很好，我们都很愉快。我对他们说，你们对我太 nice 了，谢谢呀。C. D. 说："你正是我们等待的人！"这话到今天依然给我以温暖和力量。

后来她有新书出版，就会寄给我。

她曾经在葡萄牙的一个文学活动上谈到我 90 年代初在中国的经历。她演讲中没有提到我的名字，是因为当时我不愿意她提到。这篇演讲收在 2016 年 1 月铜峡出版社出版的 C. D. 散文作品集《诗人、狮子、有声图像、法罗力托餐厅、圣罗奇教堂的婚礼、大盒子商店、镜中变形、春天、午夜、火及一切》（*The Poet, the Lion, Talking Pictures, El Farolito, a Wedding in St. Roch, the Big Box Store, the Warp in the Mirror, Spring, Midnights, Fire & All*）中"那些能够付出谦和的人"（Of Those Who Can Afford to be Gentle）这一部分。

所有这一切，现在回想起来，我几乎依然不能自已……

我最后一次见到 C. D. 是在 2011 年 11 月，在北岛组织的香港国际诗歌之夜的活动上。那时她已经瘦得不行，身体明显更虚弱了。

她在 2016 年 1 月去世。享年 67 岁。

美国第二代垮掉派诗歌领袖安妮·沃德曼（Anne Waldman）曾经这样评价 C. D.：" C. D. 莱特出奇的锐敏，大度，机智，具有全景视野，意趣昂扬。她是我们中间最无所畏惧的作家之一，带着紧迫感，穿透我们时代的黑暗。她以南方人特有的见证方式，以强力创新的、时常令人叹为观止的语言，来探究历史、人性和意识。"（美国诗人学会网 Academy of American Poets 2016 年 1 月 13 日发布）

我翻译过两首 C. D. 的诗，亦收入《重新注册》。2011 年香港中文大学出版社曾经出版过薄薄的一册中英双语对照的 C. D. 诗集《火焰》（*Flame*，陈东飚译）。听说华东师范大学出版社也将出版一部 C. D. 莱特的诗集。甚感欣慰。

2019年6月，我在德国柏林参加诗歌节。马其顿诗人尼古拉·玛兹罗夫（Nikola Madzirov）告诉我，弗罗斯特·甘德书写C. D. 和他自己的诗集《相伴》获得了普利策诗歌奖。

后来读到了青年诗人、译者李栋发来的《相伴》的原文和译文。李栋曾常年生活、学习于美国和德国，曾是C. D. 和弗罗斯特在布朗大学的学生。C. D. 去世以后，他在德国编过一本收入了多国诗人作品，用英、德、汉三种语言出版的悼念C. D. 的诗集。现在他把弗罗斯特的《相伴》翻译成中文出版，这对弗罗斯特、对中国的诗歌读者，对作为弗罗斯特的读者的我，或许也对冥冥中的C. D.，都是一件大事。

2019年5月，弗罗斯特曾在上海1862时尚艺术中心朗诵，当时《南方人物周刊》的记者李乃清对他做过一个长篇访谈《诗歌是探索心灵的新闻纪实》。在这篇访谈中，弗罗斯特透露，多年中他和C. D. 互为第一读者。他说："这本《相伴》是我写的第一部没有她相伴的诗集。2016年1月她突然离世，此后一年半时间我什么也写不出来，直到渡过那段艰难的痛苦时期，我才重新提笔写作。"弗罗斯特的《相伴》是一本与爱、生命、死亡相对称的诗集。

中国诗人们除非写长诗，一般很少围绕一个主题写一本诗集。我们当然知道组诗的概念，我们也可以说甘德的《相伴》是一个超大组诗。他的这本书令我想起英国诗人泰德·休斯为亡妻西尔维娅·普拉斯写下的《生日来信》。在《相伴》中，弗罗斯特幽幽地说话，自言自语，既是私密性的，又向黑暗敞开。有时候黑着黑着就见到了光亮。作者说话时，另一个人仿佛就坐在他身边。

这些诗歌有一种表面缓缓流动的感觉，就像水知道自己流过树枝、岩石和旧胶鞋。作者的悲伤是被控制住的。他进入感觉和书写的细节之中，似乎只有这样，倾听者才会满意。

在这本诗集中，弗罗斯特的语言和形式依然是实验的，但他的实验较从前更加内化。换个说法，实验已经内化于弗罗斯特的写作，已然成为一种自然的书写。这书写不仅是形而下的，也是形而上的。在《第一首叙事诗：花环》中他说：

如此炽烈的爱　　把两人缠绕
两人拥有同一声音　　世界的全部
爱愈是同一　　就愈有爱

这里，词汇轻轻落地，变成了花朵。它们揪住我们，变成我们的精神财富。

2020 年 3 月 10 日
新冠肺炎疫情期间

I thought you were an anchor in the drift of the world;
　　　　　but no: there isn't an anchor anywhere.
There isn't an anchor in the drift of the world. Oh no.
I thought you were. Oh no. The drift of the world.

　　　　　　　　　　　— William Bronk

BE WITH

The political begins in intimacy

SON

It's not the mirror that is draped, but
what remains unspoken between us. Why

say anything about death, inevitability, how
the body comes to deploy the myriad worm

as if it were a manageable concept not
searing exquisite singularity. To serve it up like

a eulogy or a tale of my or your own
suffering. Some kind of self-abasement.

And so we continue waking to a decapitated sun and trees
continue to irk me. The heart of charity

bears its own set of genomes. You lug a bacterial swarm
in the crook of your knee, and through my guts

writhe helminth parasites. Who was ever only themselves?
At Leptis Magna, when your mother & I were young, we came across

statues of gods with their faces and feet cracked off by vandals. But
for the row of guardian Medusa heads. No one so brave to deface those.

When she spoke, when your mother spoke, even the leashed
greyhound stood transfixed. I stood transfixed.

I gave my life to strangers; I kept it from the ones I love.
Her one arterial child. It is just in you her blood runs.

BECKONED

At which point my grief-sounds ricocheted outside of language.

Something like a drifting swarm of bees.

At which point in the tetric silence that followed

I was swarmed by those bees and lost consciousness.

At which point there was no way out for me either.

At which point I carried on in a semi-coma, dreaming I was awake,

avoiding friends and puking, plucking stingers from my face and arms.

At which point her voice was pinned to a backdrop of vaporous color.

At which point the crane's bustles flared.

At which point, coming to, I knew I'd pay the whole flag-pull fare.

At which point the driver turned and said it doesn't need to be

your fault for it to break you.

At which point without any lurching commencement,

he began to play a vulture-bone flute.

At which point I grew old and it was like ripping open the beehive
    with my hands again.

At which point I conceived a realm more real than life.

At which point there was at least some possibility.

Some possibility, in which I didn't believe, of being with her once more.

EPITAPH

To write *You*
existed me
would not be merely
a deaf translation.

For there is no
sequel to the passage when
I saw—*as you would*
never again
be revealed—you see me
as I would never
again be revealed.

Where I stand now
before the throne of
glory, the script
must remain hidden. Where,
but in the utterance itself?

Born halt and
blind, hooped-in by
obligations, aware
of the stare of
the animal inside, I
hide behind mixed
instrumentalities
as behind a square
of crocodile scute—

while cyanide drifts
from clouds to
the rivers. And in this
too might be seen
a figuration
of the human,
another intimately
lethal gesture of our
common existence.

Though I also wear
my life into death, the
ugliness I originate
outlives me.

DEADOUT

Gets out his dab rig and shatter
At once at its mercy and in control of it

The bull snake lifted the terrarium cover
About three feet six from snout to vent

Youngbloods metaphorizing death
What kind of clue do they have

Her scent: vinegar, zinc oxide, and hinoki cypress
He dreamed of it awake dreams of it

Watching another season of Spanky Wankers
Only made his fillings ache

So now he's got reptile dysfunction
Me too, says the dust.

Motorcycle parked in the handicapped spot
He regards the forest of standing dead snags

II.

Youngbloods metaphorizing death
Only made his fillings ache

The bull snake lifted the terrarium cover
He dreamed of it awake dreams of it

Gets out his dab rig and shatter
Me too, says the dust

About three feet six from snout to vent
So now he's got reptile dysfunction

Her scent: vinegar, zinc oxide, and hinoki cypress
At once at its mercy and in control of it

What kind of clue do they have
He regards the forest of standing dead snags

Watching another season of Spanky Wankers
Motorcycle parked in the handicapped spot

.

CARBONIZED FOREST

The eye that was open on Friday.

The portent and the portent's flensed hide. Ribbons of flesh

swarming downward. Like a school of leeches

deserting some unlit cataclysm.

And a briary phantom there, Stygian, erect.

Saying, here is the untranslation of the world.

Mounted on a spire of form.

The disembarkation of abyss. Fragmentary sputtering.

And what you thought were dark whiptails of illumination

were bristles from a shaved bear

being milked for bile in a rusting cage. Nested

among the mesh of soft translucent sounds

fallen from your lips, the

vestiges of someone's breathing.

ENTENDERMENT

You could see: her   consciousness was in her skin
While his primary material   was weightlessness
She candled   eggs for Petaluma Poultry
And daydreamed   of stars glowering
In the Prawn Nebula's ultraviolet light
He saw himself   a victim of place
Among shirtless gods   playing frisbee on the green
Oh death, he mumbled (in his sleep), I'm   coming for you
It's true, la vida   es caprichosa y puñetera
Full of unresolved sevenths   and ninths
So like Su   Hui's infinite poem

And once when sipping   water he coughed,
She started to   laugh, mistaking his gesture
Every event drags   loss behind it

Dark, be bright
There's nightshade in my brain

They meant to shut their door   to the setting sun
But her knees   poked through the soap bubbles
While he stayed out late   lying on his back
Under the ultraviolet light of the Prawn Nebula

Behind   a drawn curtain
The nurse   cursed
Giving voice   to his own inarticulacy
Trauma   brings its singular sharpness.
Everyone sees her   in his eyes

He offers a cigarette   for the dog to eat
And goes back   to metronoming

Re-coupled   to the common lag of friends
Tic Tacs   rattle in his pocket
He's breathing tequila   fumes at 9 a.m.
Unreadable but not   ambiguous
Like hounds   yowling at the horizon
Below the Prawn Nebula's ultraviolet light

She wrote, *Life*   *feels life in language*
Her mind's voluptuousness   so substantial
Adjectives   fizz away
He observes   the shadow thrown
By nothing is thrown   by the nothing he is

MADONNA DEL PARTO

And then smelling it,
feeling it before
the sound even reaches
him, he kneels at
cliff's edge and for the
first time, turns his
head toward the now
visible falls that
gush over a quarter
mile of uplifted sheet-
granite across the valley
and he pauses,
lowering his eyes
for a moment, unable
to withstand the
tranquility—vast, unencumbered,
terrifying, and primal. That
naked river
enthroned upon
the massif altar,
bowed cypresses
congregating on both
sides of sun-gleaming rock, a rip
in the fabric of the ongoing
forest from which rises—
as he tries to stand, tottering, half-
paralyzed—a shifting
rainbow volatilized by
ceaseless explosion.

ON A SENTENCE BY FERNANDA MELCHOR

¿Qué es lo más cabrón que te ha pasado en la vida?
The most fucked-up thing to happen to me?
Addled by busyness, I crumpled my life and let it drop
and then I outlived my life, rocking
on my misery like a cypress in the wind. I watched
stars emerge from a black egg. Lucidity
of loss. Someone came to tell me the spider
vibrating on its long legs in the ceiling corner
over my desk doesn't exist now. It is wedged
between the violent uninterruptedness
of one single day and the void I discovered
inside myself. Forehead tautening with self-pity.
I said, You think you know me, but you don't
know me from Adam's goat. And she said,
I do, and you are one and the same thing.

STEPPING OUT OF THE LIGHT

Bleaching the
spaces between
each trunk, fog delineates,
from
a vast of green,
the silhouette of
each pine
on the slope.

Maybe it's like that,
only all along it was
obscured by what?
Rush, distraction? Fog.
A pine. Querying
grosbeak. Something
shifts. You find
yourself in another
world you weren't
looking for where
what you see is that
you have always been
the wolves
at the door. Left

ajar, gaping, your own
door. And you burst
in as the Mangler,
you gouge out
your right eye which
hath offended. And you

burst in as the Great
Liar gorging
on your own flesh
and as Won't
Let Go who shreds
your tendons, gnaws
your femur. You can't
stop bursting in,
coming upon yourself
alone, vulnerable, in the
privacy of your dying,
bending to pick up
with a tissue a crushed spider

from the bedroom floor,
half-sensing in your solar
plexus the forces
of that which cannot yet
be sussed, discovering yourself
once again already
to have been inside something
like an equation with
a remainder, a deodand, a
reminder of the impossibility
of reconcilement—
to what? Once again. Forgive
yourself, they say, but
after you forgive
what you have lived,
what is left? You can't

set aside the jigger
of the present from
the steady pour of hours
or even differentiate
trails of ants
scurrying through some
massive subterranean network
from the shredded
remains of a galaxy
backlit by star glow. Time

to close the door you think
but your face is changed,
so many crow's feet. You
must be on
to the next stage
in which you begin
to recognize
your mortal body,
that nexus of your various
holds on the world, as
repository of every-
thing you didn't know
you took in, human
and not, all of it
charged and reactant
which accounts for the trembling
in your hands as now
you discern the
body of your body—

like a still,
hanging bell
that catches and concentrates
each ghostly, ambient
reverberation.

WHAT IT SOUNDS LIKE

As grains sort inside a schist

An ancient woodland indicator called *dark dog's mercury*

River like liquid shale

And white-tipped black lizard-turds on the blue wall

For a loss that every other loss fits inside

Picking at a mole until it bleeds

As the day heaves forward on faked determinations

If it's not all juxtaposition, she asked, what is the binding agent?

Creepy always to want to pin words on "the emotional experience"

Azure hoplia cockchafer, the caddis worm, the bee-louse, blister beetle, assassin bug

The recriminations swarm around sunset

When it was otherwise quiet all the way around

You who were given a life, what did you make of it?

WHERE ONCE A SOLID HOUSE

The voice singing in the kitchen   isn't your voice
There is   no voice singing in the kitchen

Opens last night's   pizza box
Its dry   strings of cheese splayed
Like tendons   in a crushed hand

From your deep I've spilled   into shallows
Flopping   asphyxiated
My speech   a paroxysm

How I wish   you are here
As I try   to gather the periphery
The places that impressed   themselves on us and
It all returns   strangely as fog
Rising just to flatten   under the bridges

When you asked for less   rigor more entenderment
When you asked   for more—

Knowing: not as recitation   but as
The unhinging   somatic event
Though now all   my memories begin with outcomes
As in Ferdowsi's   *Shahnameh*
Our annals blend into landscapes   where they took place
The protagonists so loose   their molecules mix
With swaths   of water with earth and light

For *surely the people*   *is grass* like they say
Even here   at Punto de las Culebras
No bitterness   no envy no greed

Unless   this is something else altogether
Akin to turning leaves   with a stumpripper only
To find a   striking pit viper

THE SOUNDING

What closes and then
luminous? What opens
and then dark? And into
what do you stumble
but this violet
extinction? With
froth on your lips.
8:16 a.m. The morning's
sleepy face

rolls its million
eyes. Migrating flocks
of your likesame species
incandesce
into transparency.
A birdwatcher lifts

her binoculars. The con-
tinuous with or without
your words
situates you here
(here (here)) even while
you knuckle your eyes
in disbelief. Those

voices you love (human
and not), can you
hear their echoes
hissing away like
fiery scale
from an ingot hammered
on some
blacksmith's anvil?
And behind those
voices, *what is that*
blowing
the valves of your ears open
as black rain,
not in torrents, but
ceaselessly comes
unchecked out of everywhere
with nothing
to slacken it.

FIRST BALLAD: A WREATH

after St. John of the Cross

In the beginning the Word   was as being
In happiness   infinitely the Word possessed

The same Word being was   said to be beginning
Beginninglessly   it went on

A sum caroming   through fervid void
For the Word   from the outset

Always was   conceiving
Concentrating its   consequence for

Glory in the Word   possessed the being
And all of being's substance it   gleaned from the Word

Lover in beloved in   the other one went on
And that love which entwined them   was of the same

Sum two   voices one beloved
Among two   and in them each

One happiness   rendered them one lover
A splendor un-   confessed—gleaming

As two possess one being   each alone possessed it
Each of them in love   a plenum of the Word

Whose being each   twined around the other
Beyond comprehension   an ineffable knot

Such fervid love   entwined the two together
In one voice both possessed   a plenum of the world
The more that love was one   the more of love there was

ARCHAIC MANO

In (microscopic) pocks of a
palmsize basalt stone
traces of green corn purslane
(snakefat) and piñon fuse
with smeared roots
and beeweed pollen
(ochredust) which drifts
summerlong into the
scalp of a woman kneeling
(intent) and bent over a
lightbitten stone basin
her muscles flexed
trapezius to
triceps the wrist   *(thin like yours)*
working a short
orbital swipe hand-
stone taking
the curve
of palm (cupped)
and her torso's weight
fallingthrough while
swallows dive and
veer along the sheer
cliff the warm
scabbed heel of her
palm bears down
(heel of palm) onto
and into the skirlingsound
stone merged
with the hand

        that grinds it
        wheel-wise,
          the maker (breathblown)
          alive
            in her tool (lithe)
              flies fuss and
              land her hair
              falling across her

(as your hair)   eyes radiant-   *(across your eyes)*
              upbeat leaftrilled and
          into this cadence
        is inset
        the slower cadence
      to which
      she rocks her baby
       when he cries
        and all the variable
          tempos of her breath,   *(breathe)*
          her body's measure
            countless (breaths)
              decibels of fullness
              daysutterance and
            stress all this
              pressed (against basalt),
              vesicles into the stone

                into the (pocked) stone

                    goes a rabbit hair
                    brushed from the hand
                    that scraped
                    the hide in late
                    eyelong afternoon when
                    red ants pour from
                    holes in rocky soil
                    ticking across fluff grass
                    (square-headed ants) toward
                a garden where three
            turkeys peck those (leaf-
            eating) ants (so that
                the garden greensup)
                a minor victory
                    that registers
                        in the eyes   *(and behind her eyes)*
                            of the woman   *(your eyes)*
                        who scuffs
                        stone on stone
                    in the floodbuckling
                    blare of violence
                and time
                that pockets her light
            in my (our) light
            as my pupil narrows
                in its lens and I bend   *(lord, I kneel)*

in a clearing
(before your stone) to pick up
and weigh this density
hawkglide wingspread
my hand holding what
millennia ago
her hand held
who winks out as
I come clear (to
whom?) on a
green hillside
where someone kneels
in the now (even
now) beyond
our (stillflow) looking

TELL THEM NO

"The essence of the thing is often in the flash." —Clarice Lispector

Like some
freshly emergent
thing, he clung
to her
until the chitin
of his
limbs hardened
and fluid
flowing
from his eyes
and through the
struts of his
wings crystallized.

What a good
human life
looks like. In
bed as
out. An extreme
conjunction.

When I first wet
and swirled in its
cream the sheeny
badger-hair
shaving brush you
gave me as a gift, its
shocking feral musk
locked on to my face.

Fog all morning, impressive
gray hat-band under
mottled crown of mountain,
its top edge sliding
south and thin
steam from the Petaluma
dairy spewing in
the same direction.

Not to
choose one
happiness over
another but to
keep choosing
an Appomattox
unhappiness?

Stumbling again
dumbly
home into the
line of my
own questioning.

Carried too far
off course? As
when the caterpillar
carrying wasp
maggots turns
to wasp maggots
currying
the caterpillar's
corpse.

So hard—no
matter how bad
expressed—
your own or
other's pain,
undressed—to
        turn from.

The cabinet
door's squeaky
dactylic remark:
Hap-pi-ness?
But each morning
the same
scene. A lizard
doing push-ups
on the same
baked rock.
My unsalvable
inclination for
daily routine.

Not far
from the right
metaphor:
a cigar coming
apart in the train
station toilet.

A lo que una buena
vida humana
se asemeja. Una
conjunción extrema.

She said suffering wasn't necessary.
He said it was the gateway.
She said, Drag it back where it came from.
She said, You call everybody baby.
He said, It's like free money, sort of.
She said he said to just stand here.

It means just
what it feels like
it means.

Their dog's deep gaze,
her stomach gurgling.
Clitoris plumping under pressure.
Was that a pump knot on his forehead?
Long doctor-office afternoons
drained her life. Hummingbird?
His suede jacket went dark at the collar
with oil from her hair.

Then scratched my
arm with my teeth,
nicking the cap
of the eggshell and
taking the larvae
of recognition into
my mouth.

To parcel it
out, the self
as introduction.
Who am I *is*
what I can do.

At some point, change
results in a retrogression
the mind sees
as failure. A disgusting
odor cultivated. So
I search for your
face with a file-like
roughness as though
for a resonant edge.

At his solar
plexus, the
elevator
cable snaps.
It's when I lie
down at night,
she says,
my heart
races.

The flowers I
pick too
late hiss
in the vase,
missing you.

When what is
demanded is
change so
fundamental
only another
personality could
accomplish it.

What blind gnawing
mandibled head
was chewing up the silken
thread we thought
would guide us
back to bed?

Are you
hyperventilating?
she calls
from the next
room.

Pasted-on
conversational
replies.

It lopes and turns,
lopes and turns, lopes
and turns to look
back toward the
road where
she stands
immobilized, as
though watching.

Is there nightshade
in my brain? That
I conceive
your consequence
as some stage in
my need?

Dear spider, in
this house eight
legs are too many.

A few days later
their bliss grew
an impenetrable
skin. Then dissolved
itself completely,
the liquid content of
that skin turning
to a sort of jelly
from which erupts
a new creature
whose organs
lack any identity
with what came
before.

Have I lived
something stupid?
Am I the coward
responsible for
nothing?

Suspended
between north
and south,
claims to ex-
perience pain,
and so
sustains
an orchestral
tension.

Saturation point.
When your own misery preens
you against the misery
of others.

Keeps his hat on as
he enters, but thoughtfully
wipes his feet. The women
at the far table are carpenters
wearing kneepads. On the
room's near side,
a rough caste of men
sit conspiratorially close
and track each other
from the corners
of their eyes. Contagious
guffaws punctuating
brief jokes.

At the bar, honey
bottle in a bowl of
water. *Account
of the ants*. Sign
says Hangovers
Installed & Serviced.

Standing in a wind of
diesel fuel waiting
for his luggage. Shaking
silently, mouth agape.
Pulping his eyes
with his knuckles.

The spectacularization
of the trivial, bad
faith hilarity, the
imitation of the imitation's
imitation intensifying
the suck of a vacuum.

I hear the busyness in
their voices, they hear
the busyness in my voice.
To be oblivious, in some
manifold danger. And
so one lives.

Like how
early around?
she asked.

Here is a steel wire with a ring at one end.
Intuition of the infinite.
At its other end I've screwed a conical cap
with sharp cutting edges at the base.
The infinite always intuited against
the background of the infinite. If
it doesn't serve to open up
a sound, the particular sound for
instance of my lips releasing
your name, then a gland may be involved
and another kind of treatment
called for. Won't you please
toss a handful of your infinite
phosphene into my gloom-sopped eyes.

A copper-iridescent laughter finishes up your sentence.

This last, contemporary stage,
my stage, the stage that anticipates,
that counter-actualizes my
contingency here, my under-
regarded privilege, this stage
will reach its maturity today
causing a slight rise
in temperature followed by
inflammation around the throat
and jaw where numerous red
nodules swell with serous
fluid. Doc's advice: *Don't probe*
them with your fingertips. Even the
greatest care proves insufficient.

Didn't lose
his own but
found another
voice that
didn't fit.

"If you want
to throw in
some dirt," the priest
addressed the widower
and his child generally
but did not
complete
the sentence.

Carrying
the rat of
affliction between
my teeth for
all to see. Just.
Try. To. Take. It.
From. Me.

His readiest emotion
was righteousness. Self-
absorbed error. But
now it's terror.

Siphon the real
into the practical: that's
what the drugs do.

Field flecked purple with nightshade
and lupine. Ruby-throated bird
at the bottlebrush bloom. One's
own mediocrity sharpens it.

Dog baying in tune
with the siren. Maybe the
couple will arrive yet
in time for events
to assign them
another meaning. As
she disengages the hooks
from the eyelets, he stiffens.

EVAPORACIÓN: A BORDER HISTORY

Paisanos they call
    roadrunners, brothers of the land. A dozen
Mexican corpses marooned
        under desert sun.
In cottonwoods by the river,
zone-tailed hawks squeal. Visible
    desde el aire, the craquelure of
an abandoned runway
          overlies
        toxic waste and unexploded munitions.
    Bordered by purple and yellow
bloomstalks: lechuguilla.
        Volcanic chimneys up-thrust
            from barren flats. Agleam
    in a basalt outcrop, fist-size
            feldspar crystals. The old raiding trails
    from Comanchería convergen
en un path packed by hoofprints.

Alarming *ki-dear ki-dear* of a
Cassin's kingbird on the
barbed fence. 150 miles
surveilled by a white aerostat
que se parece a una ballena. Between those peaks
sits Panther Laccolith. Both vaqueros
staked out naked, screaming on an ant hill.
Female katydid waving her foreleg tympanum
at the stridulating males. The fine-
grained intrusion that veined the mountain
also silled Paint Gap Hill.
Su caballo tembla en agonía, pinned to the ground by a spear.
Hovering over the field, a flock of crested flycatchers.
The border-patrol dog lifts its leg
at the tire of the Skywagon. Cercas de coachwhip
van paralelas al camino. Chihuahua
Trail following Alameda Creek. They call it
horse-crippler cactus.

Vietnam-era seismic probes
enterrados bajo estas propiedades privadas. Lava-rock
rims the sides.
Give it a break, mockingbird.
El Despoblado. Giant yucca and bunch grass.
And what ventures into the afternoon heat? Only Pharoah ants.
Only the insulated darkling beetle.
En los dos lados del pavimiento, magnetic sensors
registran movimiento y dirección. Evening
cicadas eclipse tree crickets.
A thousand head of cattle
driven below the trachyte hoodoos. It nibbles
a prickly pear: cottontail at dusk.
Human contraband at dusk. Famous
for their dwarf fauna, estos estratos fósiles. Depositions of
carnage, catches
of light. Our legacy
mission. A carcass of
the unspoken
aullando.

RUTH

Her husband lifeless
in chair facing
TV, whole days
mute, her own mind,
her hearing,
shot. *And it won't
get any better. Absolutely
nothing to look
forward to,* she says
to whom if
not you?

Wearing two identical
left shoes. *No one*
believes I don't
dye my hair, she remarks
for the umpteenth
time. Point taken, I'm
grayer than my
mother though
in the mirror I see
her face, her small
dark eyes.

Five states north, he
wonders what
causes the
swishing
he hears behind
his mother's
voice: she's
down on the
floor, the phone
in one hand
and with
the other,
she must be
scratching the
tumorous dog
whose paw
convulsively
rakes the carpet.

green case on the nightstand
glasses on a Redskins lanyard

green glasses case
containing one hearing aid

minus its battery on the nightstand
glasses on a Redskins lanyard

in the green grass
under one of many bird feeders

in the backyard thronging
with blurred mute birds

Occasional muculent chortling
or choking and steady
beep of the EKG.

The beak-hard
determination to
be a good person,
what happened
to that? How
is it true
I have to
go now? She's lost
my name, but the
occasion of my
presence begs
more. Who is my
mother now I am
unspoken for?

So take her hand, walking in
the garden: an animal moment of warmth
she won't recall after our sit. Voracious
starlings ride a swinging cage of suet.
That signal enthusiasm in her eyes
muddles with torment. Choose whatever
you will and the disease
still wins. Like a heavy shawl,
the shadow of cloud drags across
mountains on the horizon. Maybe I've
misread her expression.

To plunge into love as into a sidewalk.
Came awake as though I were a siren going off.
The ghastliness of putting food in my
mouth, my belly gurgling
like so many horse-leeches. And so
days-to-come will crack open without you,
dropping their yolk over places you walked.
And the white lowly primrose will foam
wild like some scrap of your happiness
refusing to abandon me. Blah blah. The
mirror in the shrine is memory. All
you lived adjusts now and is lived back
in me here on earth. A flock of geese
sifts through the barrow pit. Post-puke
acid sears my throat.

To find the present breaking itself
loose from the sequence of events, bolting
through gaps in the corral of context and
carrying its befuddled rider

                             into an expanding plain of brumous outlines.

◆ ◆ ◆

How she fights the sleeping pill, to stay up with me as I drive back
from the beach, to keep talking, to speak and be spoken to: the
assurance of voices, even her own now druggy iterative slur which is
like low birdsong, a blind inquiry in twilight— *is someone there?* —and a
claim she is alive, here in the seat beside me, her seatbelt around her
as she overcomes the pill, the devious obstacle course, the drowsiness
I administered in order to drive her four hours home this evening,
to concentrate on driving, to save my pollen-swollen and mucus-
inflamed throat from the overtime shift of talk, to stay the repetitive
questions, her struggle among scraps and familiar names torn
from faces and feelings, the cipher-names of her husband and her
grandchildren, a language of blanks, I drive with my left hand on the
wheel, the other massaging the loose skin of *her* hands, feeling for
the tightened cords in her palms, bands of fascia that curl her fingers
forward, and when I think she's finally fallen asleep, her face up-tilted
and drawn, as we cross Indian River Inlet where she'd often, with
my father, fished for flounder from the Grady-White whose single
outboard, pumped and primed, they'd startled into coughs of blue
smoke in the canal back in Bethany hours earlier and piloted through
the gauntlet of buoys— *red right return* —that drew it through Assa-
woman Bay, past Harpoon Hanna's, and into the yawning Atlantic—
when I start to pull my hand away, she tightens her grip, not opening
her eyes, maybe in reflex, holding on to her will to be awake with
me, her son, whom she knows, whom she thanks now in her almost
sleep, her narcotic fatigue, in the spreading murk of the pill I coaxed
her to swallow so that the trip might be easier while she rides beside
me, holding on.

◆ ◆ ◆

Sitting on the edge of the bed with her shirt and pants off, she reaches behind to unclasp her bra. I help her stand and draw her underwear down, and she lists to one side in pain, though she doesn't complain.

This is how she wants to go to the bathroom, naked, before we put her pajamas on. Never either shy or proud of her body. Even in my childhood, I understood she regarded the body as implement. Whatever the psychological traumas my sisters and I metabolized, we grew up at ease in our bodies, unembarrassed by nakedness.

Before me, my mother looks plumper than she does in clothes, but staggering toward the bathroom, reaching for the doorknob, she is a splotched drama of mortality, her buttocks collapsed into folds, the scar from her vertebroplasty lost in a constellation of liver spots, her waist overcome by sagging flesh.

A memory: in La Paz, I saw the old Aymara wave backwards over their shoulders when they spoke of the future. And to reference the past, make sweeping forward motions with their hands. The Aymara word for eye, front, and sight signals *past,* while the word for *future* means back or behind. In my mother's body, too, her front is the past and her back, the future.

She sits and I bunch pajama-bottoms over her feet, one at a time, and pull them up as she bends forward to stand in elaborate slow motion. Another world's wounded crane.

◆ ◆ ◆

To listen to each repetition with renewed attentiveness as if it were the first occasion, to forget you've heard it before and to receive her words as her first words or her last ones, for she repeats things not only because she's forgotten but also so they will be remembered. To come into a rhythm of farewell with her, marking it, relishing its periodicity, in order to crack open another kind of love inside the old, familiar love, a vast of acceptance, without condition, akin to what a mother might feel for her child.

◆ ◆ ◆

Want to but can't. I can't die, she says, and her eyebrows
furrow, expatiating the point. A chiming
of patient monitors like electronic crickets
in perpetual night. Or a subaltern intelligence. Code
red is clear. Did Karin put lipstick on you this morning?
A quarter turn of the petcock on the O_2 tank. We brought
dinner from The Quotidian Pain. Outside
the hospital window, stars glowing in the ultraviolet
light of the Prawn Nebula. *It's you who are*. What?
A hummingbird, she says. My lord, in heart, and let
the health go round. Though I am so far already
in your gifts.

LITTORAL ZONE

Entrance

Whether the blackness is interior—pelagic & vegetal there, organic & intestinal there—or mere background for such shapeliness of globes: spangled with lampyrid glow, airy with striate foliation, and nowhere stricked-off level.

The shapes are white as tissue? Gauze?
No, they are transparent and white.
They are membranous?
They are milky.
And the vertical thrust of their entanglement?
Shows they coalesced under the influence.

Suspiration from our
lung-thicket. Lengths of
limbs in limbo on
the furrowed sheets:
so love buds again, a-
gain in trembles above
this earth-smoke.

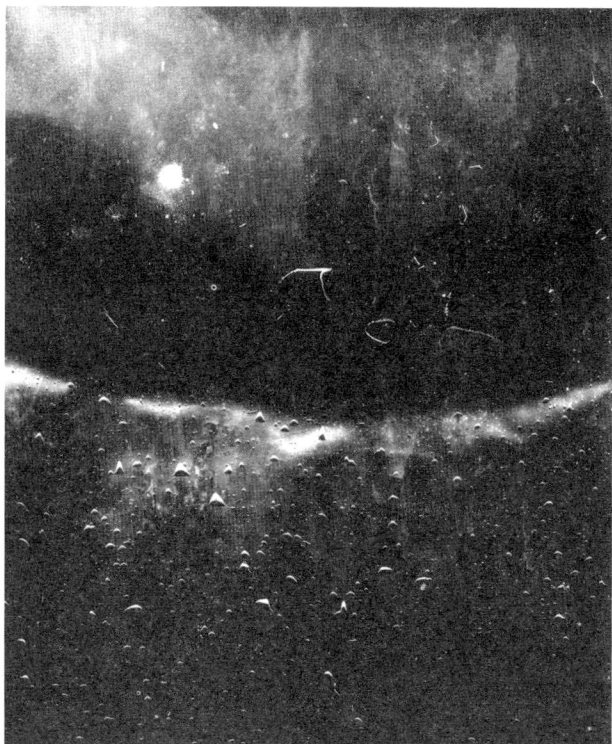

Exit

A swarm of projectile bobbles lifts (effervescent) over the lip into a
grim rictus and drifts there, lost along the spackled backwall.

*Such light, like ivory spokeshaves flared. And knobby florets caroming
radially over the curve, the curve extremetizing distance, distance weighing
against foreground. Were such improvisation to rise spontaneously out of
itself, with whom might it be shared?*

Fuegos fatuos: we cast
double shadows in Pantone
blacks. My salamandrine
longing stutter-caught
on your nocturnal gorges.
Until you're sub-
tracted from the visible
escarpment and I'm a throbbing
waste-heap of ghost.

Entrance

They cruise white mesas moored in night, bumping opalescent
dripstone. Cave onyx. No apparent source of light.

Struck by the pointlessness of comparison, but what more can one want?
For seeing not to degenerate into habit? And what if the demands for
another kind of seeing cannot be regarded as what we take to be "seeing?" As
one turns away, the retained image vitiates what swings into view.

My levorotatory isomers
going optically active, erotic. Sweeping
across pelagic intimations, your
apprising glance: entwined
stalks, we swale against the wall.
My fingers nest in your hollow:
a flotsam of hieroglyphics
in tadpole murk.

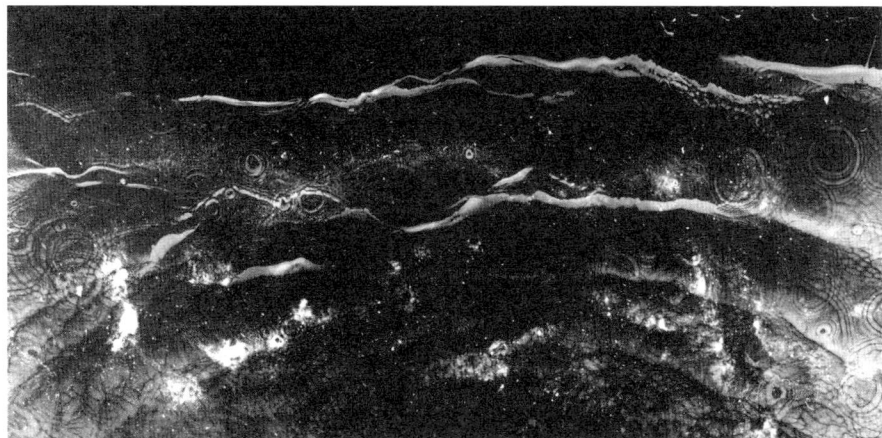

Exit

Boles, water circles, barnacle scars, the radiant circles clash, wrinkling a skin, a skin over what? The involute dimension surges from labradorite sheen, a wave-shadow scarred with cracks, and the lit edge sputtering vapor.

If a mountain lion could speak, who wouldn't understand her? On the
path, yellow jackets and Painted Ladies alight where a seep darkens loam.
A gleam on the slickensides. Sanctified stone.

The siren's sound
surrounds us at
the siltation
zone while
lightning delineates
pleats of night. Then
the sting: I'm
paralyzed, you've
disappeared. Only
my eyes. Eyes. Widening.

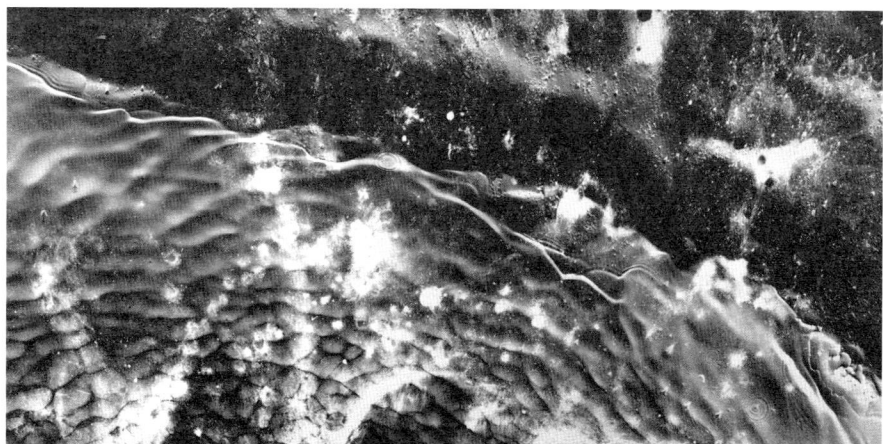

Entrance

Glacéed by fervor of sun, a carbonized melt. Granular at the liquid
edge. A shoreline cuffed with foam along dark cordilleras.

And what experience corroborates this image? Is it measured in centimeters
or miles? Or does the expression of measurement depend upon some metaphor?
Assuming there exists a place that corresponds at all. But what if there never
were such "place" and it was always modes of exchange, like months later
paying for a funeral?

The reach of neural
conduct nears
threshold momentums
in your breath, our
pooled smolder. Un-
sodden bloom: inversion
puddle. Just our wet
flesh saves us
from the scorch
of annunciation.

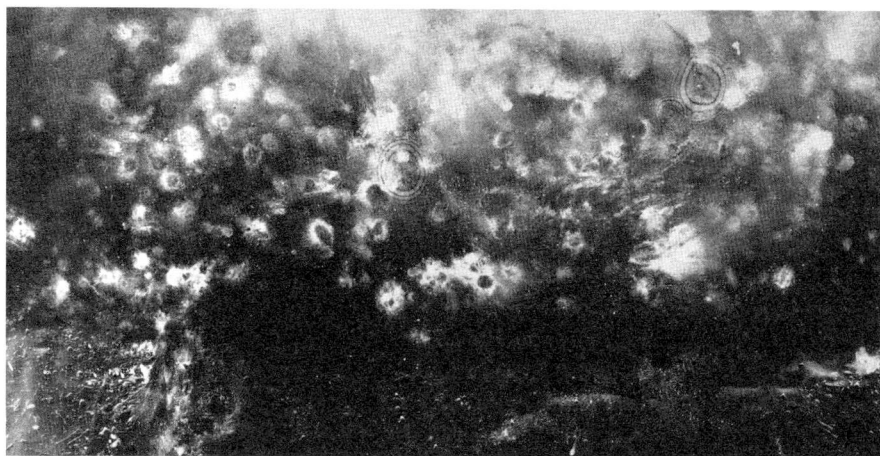

Exit

Mobbed phosphorescence, gaseous swarm. And breathbeats blazed
into an invisible integument. To begin in intimacy on this volcanic
tuff. Here to cling.

*For though we have no criterion for how to see and are not sure what we are
seeing, we are plunged into sensation. As into a novel ache. But what ever
has dispassionate description delivered?*

Your impact marks
throng the resin
of my mind. Declension,
a focal spasm. When your
eyelids release their tension,
nocturnal pods, in-
vertebrate and
membranous, surge
into my dreams. From
afar, do you see me now
briefly here in this phantasmic
standoff riding
pain's whirlforms?

ANNIVERSARY

Not, not to be known, always,
not always to be known by my wounds,

I buried melancholy's larvae
and followed you. Gathered

myself like dusk
to the black tulips of your nipples. (Tulips, tulips).

For seven days we locked the door,
we scoured the room with bird's blood.

And for a little while
in the hollow where your throat rose

from between your splendid clavicles (rose, rose),
our only rival was music,

the piano of bone-whiteness.
Nor did the light subside,

But deepeningly contracted.
The rawness of the looking.

The quiver.

A Clearing

Where are you going? Ghosted with dust. From where have you come?
Dull assertiveness of the rock heap, a barren monarchy.
Wolfspider, size of a hand, encrusted with dirt at the rubble's edge.

What crosses here goes fanged or spiked and draws its color from the ground.
Xanthic shadow at the edges.
Where are we going? Ghosted with dust. From where have we come?

Stretcher loaded with clods by a spavined work shed.
What does it mean, a cauterized topography?
One step forward and he is with us. One step back, another realm absorbs him.

The sense of epoch loosened, unstrung.
Each one thinking it is the other who recedes like a horizon.
The miraculous cage visible under his skin.

I cannot be discarded, his eyes say.
A flute that plays one note. A face.
In the open pit at noon, men waning in brightness.

I can be read, say the rocks, but not by you.
The air burnished, almost mineral, like a thin peel of mica.
Mound in the photograph, iris in the eye.

What does it mean, a cauterized topography?
To salvage rocks the color of all else from all else the color of rock.
I can be read, say her eyes, but not by you.

As if the land had abandoned itself.
Rain-flushed from denuded hills, soil powders in wind.
One step forward and we are with them. One step back, another realm absorbs us.

Don't pick up the rocks, he says, because rocks belong to the dead.
Xanthic shadow at the edges.
The distance flat as horsehair plaster, all depth sponged away.

Black knoll of tailings.
There is nothing between his eyes and ours, not even invitation.
Each stone carrying its death sentence into the animate world.

Fly maggot eating the red ant's brain.
The sense of epoch loosened, unstrung.
Light broken off in the air.

The twig's shadow has the same quality as the shadow of a man.
Glance held, an afterglow.
All depth sponged away, the distance flat as horsehair plaster.

Iris in an eye, mound in the photograph.
Don't pick him up, rocks say, because the dead belong to the rocks.
Encrusted with dirt at the rubble's edge: wolfspider the size of a hand.

A man's shadow has the same quality as the shadow of a twig.
What crosses here goes fanged or spiked and draws its color from the ground.
The air burnished, almost mineral.